HARLEQUIN®

Day Leclaire invites you to a wedding…

The Location: The Cinderella Ball.

The Groom: Jake Hondo has an inheritance to collect, but to do so he needs to wed and bed a woman—any woman.…

The Bride: Wynne Sommers is a romantic. She believes in love at first sight, knights in shining armor and that a marriage is forever. All she needs is the man to prove it.…

The Outcome: Marriage! Well, Wynne is nothing if not optimistic and who ever said a TEMPORARY HUSBAND couldn't be persuaded to stick around?

And it could be your own!

On one very special night, single people from all over America come together in the hope of finding that special ingredient for a happy ever after—their soul mate. The Cinderella Ball offers the opportunity for immediate matrimony: come single, leave wed. Which is exactly what is about to happen to three unsuspecting couples in Day Leclaire's magical new trilogy:

✦ FAIRYTALE WEDDINGS ✦

Titles in this series are:

November: TEMPORARY HUSBAND
December: ACCIDENTAL WIFE
January 1997: SHOTGUN MARRIAGE

Dear Reader,

I have a confession to make.... I used to devour
fairy tales. In fact, I'll still pick up my old, battered copy of
Grimm's Fairy Tales and lose myself between its pages for
hours on end. As a child I'd put myself to sleep making up
my own version of these stories—wonderful romantic tales of
princes and princesses and eternal love. So I suppose it's
only appropriate that the idea for my FAIRYTALE WEDDINGS
series came to me in a dream.

I found the premise wildly romantic—a ball thrown once
every five years for single individuals eager to find a suitable
mate. Attend, search for the man or woman of your dreams
and marry. All in one night.

I suppose that in real life the rational, intellectual part of
ourselves would stop us from behaving so impulsively.
But in our dreams, in our imaginations, in that impetuous,
sentimental part that we keep safely locked away from
cynical eyes, perhaps we can see ourselves nervously
entering the Montagues' ballroom and looking for that
perfect man or woman. We can leave reality behind. We
can waltz with our own personal Prince Charming and steal a
moonlit kiss in a secluded corner of the garden. And maybe,
just maybe, we'll find our soul mate.

So here's your invitation to attend the Montagues' Cinderella
Ball, to escape into a few hours of fantasy. Meet Jake Hondo,
a tough, no-nonsense cowboy, and Wynne Sommers, a
whimsical, soul-healing bit of mischief. Here's your invitation
to find *happily ever after*.

Love,

Day Leclaire

Day Leclaire
Temporary
Husband

TORONTO • NEW YORK • LONDON
AMSTERDAM • PARIS • SYDNEY • HAMBURG
STOCKHOLM • ATHENS • TOKYO • MILAN
MADRID • WARSAW • BUDAPEST • AUCKLAND

In memory of Robert M. Totton. We'll miss your humor, your wit and your wonderful stories. Mostly, we'll miss you just being there.

And special thanks to Cath Laing for her support, enthusiasm and hard work. You're super!

ISBN 0-373-03433-4

TEMPORARY HUSBAND

First North American Publication 1996.

Copyright © 1996 by Day Totton Smith.

Printed in U.S.A.

PROLOGUE

Towson, Maryland

WYNNE SOMMERS sat on the floor of her apartment and cupped her chin, her pale brows drawn together in thought. "Do you know what I really need, Laura?"

Her friend snorted, folding clothes into a large moving box. "Sure I know. You need to have your head examined if you still intend to go through with this ridiculous idea."

"No.... What I really need is a knight in shining armor. A protector."

Laura shoved the box to one side and glared. "Oh, for crying out loud! Why don't you just wish for Prince Charming, a palace and a million dollars while you're at it? It's just as realistic." She threw up her hands in despair. "Listen to me talking about realism, and to you of all people. A woman planning to marry a complete stranger wouldn't recognize reality if it bit her on the—"

"Yes?" Wynne questioned, amusement clear in her voice. "Bit me where?"

"Oh, forget it," Laura muttered. "Why do I bother?"

Wynne smiled, not in the least offended by her friend's bluntness. "Because you care. And in case you've forgotten, I know all about reality and being realistic. It hasn't worked for me, which is why I'm willing to give the alternative a try."

5

"I know," Laura said, contritely. "But to marry a complete stranger—"

"My point exactly. Since I *am* going to marry a complete stranger, why not pick one with all the qualities I need?"

"Because it's crazy. It's just asking for trouble." Laura's gaze grew concerned. "Please, don't do this. There has to be another solution."

"You know there isn't," Wynne said with calm finality. "I've lost my job, my apartment and I'm out of money. This is the only option left. It'll work out, you'll see."

Laura frowned. "What do you mean you're out of money?" she demanded. "What happened to your savings?"

"I spent every last penny on my ticket to the ball. I had to. It was the only way to find a husband by the end of the month."

A long silence stretched between them. Wynne knew she'd upset her friend, but she had no choice. From the moment she'd found out about the Cinderella Ball, she'd known it was the answer to her prayers. It had been a fluke that she'd seen the advertisement at all—a newspaper left at the restaurant where she'd worked, a gust of wind from an open doorway, pages of newsprint blowing to the floor and... And there it was. A small, elegant ad that had caught her eye and offered a chance of a lifetime.

The Cinderella Ball, it had read. *Find romance. Find your Prince Charming. Find the woman of your dreams. The Cinderella Ball offers the opportunity for immediate matrimony. Come to the ball single and leave happily wed*. And it had given a phone number, a number she'd called that very night. A ticket to the ball had been exorbitant, the application form detailed and thorough. But she'd apparently passed whatever investigative process they required and been accepted as a guest to the ball.

Unable to resist, Wynne crossed to the scarred dining table at the far end of the room and stared down at the thick gold-embossed envelope she'd placed on her best remaining china plate. It had arrived earlier that day, hand-delivered by a liveried messenger along with a card that read, *"The Montagues wish you joy and success as you embark on your search for matrimonial happiness."* Taking a deep breath, she opened the envelope again, removing the white velvet pouch inside.

Reverently she ran a callused fingertip over the pouch, then slid the surprisingly heavy gilt "ticket" from its nest. The metallic wafer caught the light from the overhead bulb and shimmered as though alive, flooding the drab room with a brilliant, golden promise. She'd done the right thing, she assured herself, made the only possible decision. Just holding the engraved ticket filled her with that certainty.

Laura came to stand behind her. "I'm sorry, Wynne," she said. "I didn't mean to criticize. It's just... I worry about you. You don't always see people the way they really are, and I'm afraid one of these days someone will take advantage of you."

"I guess that's all the more reason I should get married. My husband can make sure that doesn't happen."

"What if *he* takes advantage of you?"

Wynne laughed. "I wouldn't marry a man like that. That's why I'm going to the Cinderella Ball. The man I find will be special." She smiled with dreamy certainty. "He'll be good and kind, patient and loving. Strong. Fair."

"Yeah, right. A knight in shining armor. A protector."

A small frown creased Wynne's brow. "I know women aren't supposed to need protection. They're not even

supposed to want it anymore. Do you think he'll mind?
It won't be for long. Just until Mrs. Marsh is taken care
of.''

"You aren't going to tell him, are you?" Laura demanded bluntly. "Not *everything*?"

"It's only fair."

Laura planted her hands on Wynne's shoulders and
turned her around. "Listen, my friend. I'll go along with
this crazy scheme, I'll even help in any way I can. But
there's one condition."

"Only one?" Wynne teased.

"Just one. You aren't to tell him the truth until after
you're married."

"But—"

"Look what happened when Brett found out. He
ended your engagement."

Wynne grimaced. "He obviously wasn't the man I
thought he was."

"Nor was Jerry. Nor was Kevin. The minute they
found out, they both dumped you, too."

"All that means is that knights are in scarce supply
these days," Wynne insisted.

"My point exactly. So if you take my advice, you'll
pick out your knight, wed him, bed him, then tell him
the truth. That way he won't have any choice but to help
you."

Reluctantly Wynne shook her head. "I can't lie, Laura.
You know I can't."

"Fine. Just don't give him all the details. Be vague."
Laura glared. "You can be vague, I know you can. I've
seen you do it often enough."

Wynne peeked up at her friend. "I believe that's
thoughtful, not vague," she offered.

"Trust me. I know vague when I see it and you're
vague."

"Okay, but I can't lie."

"I'm not asking you to lie. Just be selective in what you tell him. I'm not joking, Wynne. I want your promise. I know how seriously you take promises. Swear to me that you'll keep your mouth shut until the ring's on your finger."

Wynne frowned, hesitant to commit to something so contrary to her nature. "I promise I won't tell him until after we're married...unless he asks." She lifted an eyebrow. "Is that good enough?"

"I guess it'll have to do." Laura sighed. "Let's just hope he's so enthralled by big green eyes and white-blond hair he doesn't think to ask too many questions."

"It'll work out, you'll see," Wynne consoled. "Why, with any luck at all, he'll be vague, too."

Chesterfield, Texas

Jake Hondo glared at his attorney—even though said attorney was also his best friend. Correction. His *only* friend. "You told me you could get that stipulation in the will overturned," he said in a furious undertone, yanking open a massive oak door reading, Dodson, Dodson and Bryant, Attorneys at Law.

Peter Bryant shrugged, practically jogging to keep up with his client. "I didn't expect your cousin to contest it. If it hadn't been for Randolph the judge might have let the condition slide. But that's not possible now. I'm sorry, Jake. I did my best."

"Your best, huh? Well, your best means that I have seven days to find myself a wife or I lose my inheritance." He thrust a hand through pitch-black hair and gritted his teeth, struggling to control his anger. "Marriage. What a joke."

"It's not a dirty word. Marriage can be quite pleasant."

"It's a state of pleasantness I've managed to avoid for thirty-five years. Why spoil a perfect record at this late date?"

"Come into my office where we can discuss it in private," Peter suggested, opening a doorway leading off the plush corridor. "Can I get you something to drink?" he asked, dropping his briefcase onto his desk.

"Only if it's a hundred proof. Dammit, Peter. What the hell am I supposed to do now? What about a temporary deal? You know, one of those marriage of convenience things?"

Peter poured two fingers of whiskey into a glass tumbler and handed it to Jake. "Assuming you could find someone agreeable, there's still one other detail you should keep in mind."

Jake swallowed the whiskey and lifted an eyebrow. "What's that?"

"I believe your grandfather's exact wording is...'wedded and bedded,'" Peter ventured to clarify as he crossed to sit behind the desk.

"I know his exact—" Jake ground to a halt, slamming his empty glass onto the oak table top. "You can't be serious! Tell me you don't mean what I think you do."

"'Fraid so. I gather your grandfather must have anticipated you'd try to create a loophole with a temporary arrangement. He hoped for a real marriage with a real wife and real kids."

Jake waved an impatient hand. "I don't give a damn what he hoped. Just explain the specifics. How the hell are they going to prove the marriage is consummated? Don't tell me they're going to have a doctor—"

"No, no," Peter hastened to assure. "Though if your cousin had his way it might have come to that. The lady's word will be sufficient."

Jake balled his hands into fists, wishing he were still young and impetuous enough to give physical expression to his fury. "Any other details I should know about?"

"Not as far as the will is concerned, no. But I did suspect Randolph might try something devious, underhanded and unfortunately legal. So I devised a counter measure." Peter smiled expansively as he pulled a thick, gold-embossed envelope from his desk drawer. "I believe this will help you find a temporary bride."

Jake raised an eyebrow. "What is it? A list of candidates?"

"Close." Peter patted the envelope. "I took the liberty of arranging for this the minute Randolph fired off his first salvo."

"Get to the point, Bryant."

"Sit down and I'll explain." He waited until Jake had complied before continuing. "Have you ever heard of the Cinderella Ball?"

"No. Nor am I in the mood for fairy tales."

"This isn't a fairy tale. Not exactly." Peter grinned. "Though it is sort of sweet."

"Please. Spare me."

"You're such a cynic," the attorney observed, then held up his hands as though hoping to calm a threatening storm. "Relax. Since you're not in the mood for a lengthy explanation, I'll give you the short version."

"Smart move."

"I heard about this ball back in my college days. It would seem a couple by the name of Montague throws one of these affairs every five years because that's how they first met—at a ball. One look and they fell madly in love. They were married by dawn the next day and have, according to them, lived in wedded bliss ever since. By holding this Cinderella Ball, they're hoping to give other couples a similar opportunity."

"Sounds like a bunch of bull," Jake stated bluntly. "I find it hard to believe anyone would be interested in attending something so ridiculous."

"You'd be surprised," Peter replied. "There are a lot of lonely people in the world. They want marriage and they want a partner who shares the same mind-set. All the 'guests' who request a ticket are investigated by a security company to weed out the psychos and weirdos. Those that pass scrutiny pay a hefty fee to attend. That alone culls the mix even further."

"So you sent in my name?"

Peter nodded. "If we hit a snag with the will, I thought this might be a viable alternative."

"Well, you're wrong." Jake stood and crossed to the liquor cabinet, pouring himself another drink. "There has to be some other way. Find it."

"As your lawyer, I'm telling you this is the only alternative. As your friend, I suggest you walk away. Forget the inheritance. Let Randolph have it."

Jake's expression hardened. "Not a chance."

"Then you must marry."

The words hung between them for a long moment. With a sigh, Jake nodded and sat down again. "Give me the details."

"By attending this ball, you're able to cut through all the usual first meeting nonsense and get right to the basics. Everyone who attends wants to marry, so it's just a matter of finding a compatible spouse, one who shares your interests. In just a few minutes you can discuss and settle all sorts of issues, from finances to children. And no one is offended by such frankness."

"They don't have time to be," Jake inserted.

Peter nodded. "Exactly."

"So I wander around this place canvasing women to see who'd be willing to marry me, sleep with me and then walk away. Is that it?"

"That's it, though I think I should warn you. The odds of finding someone who's agreeable are next to nil."

Privately Jake agreed. "And if I don't find myself a wife?"

Peter shrugged. "Then I won't make you reimburse me for the ticket."

Jake actually smiled. "Fair enough. But what about a prenuptial agreement? There's not much point in gaining my inheritance if some greedy little viper's going to snatch it away again."

"I can draw up a document. Getting her to sign it will be your problem."

A cold light entered Jake's eyes. "She'll sign it," he assured curtly. "Or she'll look elsewhere for a husband."

"Then let me also warn you that without her having a lawyer representing her interests, the legality of the document may be at issue. She could contest it."

"She won't," Jake stated with absolute certainty. "Otherwise she'll find herself grabbing hold of more trouble than she can handle. The woman I marry won't be some starry-eyed dreamer with visions of Prince Charming and fairy castles and happily-ever-afters dancing in her head. She's going to be plain, practical and levelheaded. And once the terms of the will are met, she's going to walk away without a backward glance. I guarantee it."

CHAPTER ONE

THE MOMENT WYNNE saw him, she knew she'd found her knight. If she hadn't already believed in love at first sight, she would have in that instant. He stood tall and broad and indomitable against the dusk-filled November sky, everything about him suggesting Prince Charming, fairy castles and happily-ever-afters all rolled into one.

He was, as far as she could tell, perfection.

She first noticed him as she approached the "palace," a huge mansion that rose out of the Nevada desert like a great white beacon of hope. He stood in the center of the flagstone walkway, taking in the whimsical, wedding cake design of the house with an expression of cynical disdain. Clearly he considered the overall effect pretentious.

She considered it a dream come true.

Not that she'd hold his attitude against him. Heavens, no. The man she married needed to be in touch with the real world, to have a tough, no-nonsense edge. He needed to be a match for Mrs. Marsh.

She slipped closer hoping to get a clear look at him. As though accommodating her, he turned slightly so the floodlights lining the walk stabbed across his face, revealing in brutal detail every austere plane and angle. What she saw stopped her cold. This was no Prince Charming boldly blocking the path, but a Prince of Darkness.

The man might have been hewn from solid rock, as starkly beautiful and as fatally dangerous as the desert

14

surrounding them. Hair as black as coal swept back from
a broad furrowed brow and framed high, arching cheekbones and a firm, squared jaw. His features were too
bold to be called handsome, but she didn't mind. The
harsh, craggy planes appealed to her.

He looked down then, as though surprised to find her
at his side, and lifted a dark eyebrow. She caught her
breath, captured within the austere glare of his bright
golden eyes. "Getting a jump on the competition?" he
asked, his voice reminding her of the rumble of distant
thunder.

She tilted her head to one side. "Excuse me?"

"You're looking for a husband aren't you?"

"Yes."

"Then run along inside, elf. I'm no one you'd want
to marry."

He was accustomed to instant obedience, she realized.
But he'd soon discover she didn't skitter away at the first
flash of lightning or crack of thunder—for that's what
his expression reminded her of, the threat of a fast-
approaching storm. "I need a strong man. You look
strong," she said instead.

"I need a wife to share my bed. And then, after a
brief-as-possible marriage, we go our separate ways."
He folded his arms across his chest and lifted an eyebrow.
"Is that what you want, too?"

"I want a man who likes to win," she said, evading
the question. "Someone who's a fighter."

"You waging war?"

She frowned, considering. "I guess you could call it
war. All right, yes. I'm waging war. But, I also need
someone fair and reasonable and patient. A . . . a gentle
warrior."

He laughed at that, amusement lightening his eyes,
but doing nothing to ease the hardness of his features.
"You have the wrong man," he stated and walked away.

She watched him go, taking in his easy, long-legged gait, not in the least surprised when people quickly made room for him, giving way to the stronger force. That was how he'd be with Mrs. Marsh, she didn't doubt for a minute. And though he claimed he wasn't fair or reasonable or patient, she suspected he lied. Oh, not deliberately. He wasn't the type. He just didn't see his own goodness. But she did.

"You'll do," she whispered with a wide grin. "In fact, you'll more than do."

Jake wended his way through the crowd streaming toward the mansion. One down, he thought grimly, and only a few hundred more to go. With nine or ten hours available to him, that meant he had to interview about a dozen or two women an hour. That gave him three and a half minutes per candidate. He shook his head in exasperation. This was crazy. Three and a half minutes to choose a wife. Great. Just great. What the hell could Peter have been thinking? Better yet, what the hell was *he* thinking to have gone along with such an asinine plan?

He climbed the sweeping steps leading toward the entrance hall and glanced back. His elf still stood where he'd left her, her dress a pale splash of green in the gathering dusk. Too bad she hadn't worked out. She'd been a tempting little morsel.

Unfortunately the instant he'd spotted her hovering at his elbow, he'd known she was all wrong. For one thing, she looked the type who expected a Prince Charming and fairy castles and happily-ever-afters. And for another, he found her too damned attractive. One look at all that white-blond hair tumbling into eyes the color of new spring leaves and he'd known he'd have to put a whole lot of space between them. Otherwise he'd end up slinging her over his shoulder and heading for the nearest exit. And that would never do.

He frowned, turning from the sight of her, shaking off the memory of her wide, pixielike smile. She had too open a face—mischievous, intelligent...and vulnerable. The sort of face that threatened to creep into a man's heart and soul and poison him with impossible fantasies. Fantasies he'd given up on eons ago. Fantasies that would never come true.

Besides, she was a complication he couldn't afford—not if he wanted to gain his inheritance.

A nudge from behind woke Wynne to her surroundings and she started, realizing she stood in the middle of the walkway lost in thought. She'd been picturing the sweetest of fantasies—one that involved a dark, handsome prince and a real house and children. It was a fantasy that could be hers, once she got past a certain masculine stumbling block.

She eyed the retreating back of the stumbling block in question, pleased beyond all measure when he hesitated and glanced over his shoulder in her direction. He needed her. The instinctive knowledge grew stronger with each passing moment. She'd sensed a gaping emptiness in him and knew that she could fill it, a raw hurt that she had the power to heal. He needed someone who could see the inherent goodness in his character, who wouldn't be fooled by his stormy expression and searing gold eyes and tough, independent attitude. He was a man plagued by demons, demons she could destroy.

He needed *her.*

Gathering up the long sweep of her skirt, she started toward the mansion. She didn't want to get too far behind her future husband. Heaven only knew what trouble he'd get into if she did. He might even pick the wrong woman through sheer ignorance. She grinned. Or sheer bullheadedness.

Stepping through the double doors leading inside, she stopped dead, staring around in amazement. The marble entrance hall seemed to stretch endlessly, the huge support pillars decorated for Thanksgiving with pine garland, fairy lights and white satin bows. A massive chandelier, glittering with thousands of tiny prisms, caught the setting sun and scattering a dancing circle of rainbows in joyous welcome. Twin, curving staircases on either side of the hallway led to the upstairs ballroom, joining at the top to form a perfect heart.

Wynne climbed the steps, feeling more like Cinderella by the minute. Reaching the upper landing, she joined others in a short receiving line, holding her invitation in a white-knuckle grip. All her hopes and dreams lay in this thin, gold metallic wafer. She closed her eyes for an instant and made a wish, a wish that all who came that night would find their heart's desire.

"Welcome to the Cinderella Ball."

With a start, Wynne opened her eyes, realizing she'd reached the front of the line. And standing before her was the most beautiful woman she'd ever seen.

The woman's hair was richly black, pulled away from her face and fashioned into an intricate knot. Her eyes were huge and a clear, rich amber, thick lashes shading the innate reserve that lurked in their depths. She held out her hand and offered a warm smile. "I'm Ella Montague."

"Wynne Sommers. It's a pleasure to meet you." She shook hands, gazing in open admiration. It might be interesting to look like this for a day instead of like the "pocketful of nothingness" Mrs. Marsh had once called her. Somehow she couldn't see Ella Montague allowing anyone to intimidate her, certainly not the beastly Mrs. Marsh. But then, everything had a price. Even beauty, judging by Ella's wary expression.

"I hope you enjoy yourself this evening," she murmured, taking Wynne's gold ticket and dropping it into the velvet-lined basket she held. "You're free to explore any of the rooms on the first two floors. Buffet-style dinners are laid out downstairs and the gardens are available for your enjoyment. Once you find a partner, marriage ceremonies are conducted in the salons off the main ballroom. If you have any questions or problems, there are footmen who can assist you. They all wear white-and-gold uniforms, so you can't miss them."

"Thank you," Wynne murmured and moved further down the line. An older couple stood together, their expressions as guileless as newborn infants.

"Welcome, my dear," the woman said in greeting, taking Wynne's hand in hers. "I'm Henrietta Montague. And this is my husband, Donald."

Wynne glanced back over her shoulder at Ella, a mesmerizing flame of gold in her Grecian-style gown, and then back at the Montagues. "Ella is your daughter?" she asked tentatively.

"Our one and only," Henrietta confirmed cheerfully. "A bird of paradise raised by wrens."

Wynne smiled. "I quite like wrens. They're quick, cheerful and always have something to say for themselves."

Henrietta beamed. "What a lovely description. Did you hear, Donald?"

"I heard, my sweet." He took hold of Wynne's hand and squeezed it. "Now you look around carefully tonight. Only the best for you."

"Oh, I've already found him," Wynne hastened to say. "And he is the best. The very best."

Tears glittered in Henrietta's eyes. "I'm so pleased. Much happiness, my dear. And with luck we'll see you again next year."

"Next year?" Wynne asked in confusion.

"That's when we hold our Anniversary Ball. All those who meet and wed at the Cinderella Ball are invited to celebrate their first anniversary with us."

Wynne gave a definite nod. "Then I'll see you again next year." With that, she moved into the ballroom and scanned the crowd for coal-black hair and a distinctive set of broad shoulders.

Time to find her husband-to-be.

Jake lounged against a wall and watched the crowd with weary impatience. Dammit all! Four miserable hours had passed since he'd arrived—four hours spent stampeding from woman to woman like some sort of lust-crazed bull in a field full of bashful cows. And he didn't have a single prospect to show for it. Oh, there were plenty of women, available in every shape and size. But they'd all come with a list of wants he couldn't care less about, let alone had a hope in hell of fulfilling.

And not one of them was interested in a temporary relationship.

A hard-eyed brunette approached just then. It didn't take long to discover she was more interested in the size of his bank account than in marital bliss. After two minutes of conversation he knew she'd never sign his prenuptial agreement. And after another two he managed to convince her he wasn't interested in purchasing the goods she had for sale. The instant she left, a redhead replaced her. She practically shook in her ivory heels and he suspected it took every ounce of gumption for her to even approach.

"Nikki Ashton," she introduced herself and offered her hand.

"Jake Hondo."

An awkward silence descended as she scrambled for something to say. "I—I'm looking for a husband," she finally announced.

"Really?" he murmured dryly. "What a coincidence. I'm looking for a wife."

She stared at him in dismay, bright color sweeping into her face. "Oh, I knew this would never work. Coming here was a mistake." A hint of violet glinted within the pansy-blue of her eyes. "I'm sorry to waste your time. It's just that I've never done this before. And I thought... I'd hoped—"

He released his breath in a gusty sigh, afraid that if he didn't say something nice—and quick—she might burst into tears. "You want to start over?"

She gave a forlorn little shrug. "Is there any point?"

"Could be. I'm looking for a temporary wife. You interested?"

That caught her attention. "Yes. As a matter of fact, I am." A small smile crept across her full mouth and she relaxed minutely. "I wouldn't mind a temporary arrangement in the least."

He lifted a sooty eyebrow. "You serious?"

"Very. I just need a husband long enough to convince my sister I'm happily married."

"Happy, huh?"

"Ecstatically happy." Her eyes narrowed. "You can fake ecstatic, can't you?"

"I suppose." He waited a beat before adding, "If you're willing to sleep with me."

Her mouth fell open. "Excuse me?"

"I have to be legally wedded and bedded to inherit my grandfather's property. And my wife will need to stand up in court and admit as much to the judge." He rocked back on his heels. "Can you handle that?"

He watched as she mulled it over. If she hadn't claimed she'd be interested in a temporary marriage, he'd have brushed her off. One glance had told him she'd never do. For one thing, she was too beautiful—as lovely as his little elf, though perhaps more colorful and vibrant.

If he'd learned nothing else in his thirty-five years of existence, he'd learned to give beautiful women a wide berth. For another, Nikki's soft, white hands hadn't seen a lick of work since the day she'd tumbled into this world. She'd be about as useful on a ranch as a silk-covered saddle.

Still, he was fast running out of options. He could tolerate the woman, if push came to shove. Let her sit in the parlor and look as gorgeous and helpless as she wanted, so long as she warmed his bed. Check that. So long as she warmed his bed *and* confirmed she'd done her wifely duty before the judge and various and sundry witnesses.

"Well?" he prodded.

"There's no other option?"

"No other option and no other conditions. How about you?"

"Just one other detail... In addition to my sister, I have a boss to convince. You'd have to act the part of the loving husband whenever we attend business functions together or whenever my family's around."

Damn. "Whoa. Time out. Where were you planning on conducting this ecstatically happy marriage of ours?"

"New York," she answered. "Why?"

"Because I have a ranch to run. I need my wife living with me in Texas."

She shook her head. "I need my husband living with me in New York." Her mouth tilted into a rueful smile. "This isn't going to work, is it?"

"Doesn't look like it."

"Thanks anyway." She offered her hand again. "And thanks for helping me through this. It should be easier from here on out." With that cryptic remark, she disappeared into the crowd.

"Wasn't she right for you?" a friendly voice questioned from behind.

He turned and glanced down, both intrigued and ir-
ritated to discover that his elf had reappeared. "I thought
I got rid of you earlier."

She shrugged, the graceful movement drawing his attention to the fine, sculpted lines of her neck and
shoulders, her short, layered hairstyle further emphas-
izing the most exquisite bone structure he'd seen in a
long time. She reminded him of a thoroughbred, lean
and delicate and fluid.

"I'm hard to get rid of," she replied, not in the least
offended by his gruff comment. "I'm persistent."

A small smile eased the corners of his mouth.
"Annoying."

"Tenacious."

"Pesky."

"Determined."

"Clingy."

She laughed up at him. "In that case, I'll grow on
you."

"That's what I'm afraid of," he muttered wryly.

Tilting her head to one side, she gave him a sympathetic look. "Not having any luck?"

"Not much. How about you?"

"Oh, I haven't given up yet. These things take time."

He grimaced. "Something we're fast running out of."

"Unfortunately."

She brushed a lock of hair from her eyes and peeked
up at him. To his amusement, the look held a contra-
dictory element of both caution and daring, and he
folded his arms across his chest. "Spit it out, munchkin.
What do you want?"

She took a deep breath and offered an engaging smile.
"I don't believe we've introduced ourselves. I'm
Wynne Sommers."

The name suited its owner—they each had a fey, almost arcane feel about them. "Jake Hondo," he replied with notable reluctance.

"Are you hungry?" she asked. "I'm starved. Why don't we visit the buffet table and you can tell me what it is you expect in a wife."

"We've already covered that ground," he said, a hard edge invading his tone. "I want a temporary arrangement. You want permanent."

"I prefer permanent," she said, correcting him. "But I'm willing to compromise."

His eyes narrowed. "I want someone who's not afraid of hard work. You'd blow away in the first gust of wind."

"Oh, I'm not that easy to blow away. And as for hard work..." She held out her hands, palms up. They were marred by calluses, the skin red and chapped. "I know my way around a bucket of soapy water."

He gritted his teeth to prevent an exclamation of fury. She shouldn't have hands like that. They should be like the redhead's hands, silky and white and pampered. He eyed her thoughtfully. His elf worked hard for a living. Is that why she'd come? To escape a life of drudgery? "You want a gentle warrior," he reminded. "And I'm not even close to gentle."

She gave a gaminelike grin. "Aren't you?"

"No," he said with pointed finality and turned away.

She didn't leave. Instead she stood quietly at his side and waited. Reluctantly he glanced down at her. Her dress was made of some sort of shimmery fabric, the light green an almost perfect match for her eyes. The V-neck bodice hugged her slender curves and he suppressed the savage urge to steal her away to a dark, private corner and become intimately familiar with those curves—curves, he suspected, that would prove to be a hell of a lot softer than her hands.

"You don't want me," he told her in a harsh undertone. "I'm not the right sort of husband for you."

He might as well have saved his breath. "If you won't eat with me, will you dance with me?" she asked.

Take her into his arms? Feel that pale, velvety skin beneath his hands, breathe in her scent and mold her body to his? He gritted his teeth. What the hell did she think he was made of? Stone?

"Not a chance." He bit out the words and grabbed hold of her work-roughened hand. "It's the buffet or nothing."

He towed her through the crowds, calling himself every kind of a fool for not avoiding the trap closing in around him. But he found he couldn't. Something in the way Wynne looked at him, the unquestioning faith he read in those candid green eyes made him want to take her under his wing and ensure that nothing ever harmed her. He didn't stop to analyze his reaction. He only knew that for the past four hours he'd caught distracting glimpses of her—and of the men stalking her like a pack of feral dogs. And each time he'd thought her on the verge of selecting one for a husband, it had felt as though he'd been mule-kicked square in the gut.

He was doing her a favor, he decided. He didn't know why she felt the need to go to this extreme, why she felt that marriage represented salvation, but he suspected she only saw the dream, not the reality. If he married her, she'd be free in a short amount of time. By then, she'd have realized that marriage didn't solve problems, it only added to them. And she'd be only too happy for an opportunity to escape.

His mouth tightened at his feeble attempts to rationalize a way around the truth. If he were honest, he'd admit that he cared about just two things—gaining his inheritance and having this woman in his bed. He wanted her. He wanted her silken limbs wrapped around him.

He wanted to see her in the full flush of passion. Most of all, he wanted her to continue gazing up at him the way she did, the way no one else ever had—with blatant adoration and trust.

She was a fool to assume him worthy of either. And he was a bigger fool for condoning it.

Wynne hesitated at the doorway to the dining area, staring in wonder at the feast laid out before them. "I've never seen so much food in all my life," she whispered.

Jake glanced at the damask-covered tables, piled high with every imaginable delicacy. The Montagues had spared no expense. His mouth twisted cynically. But then, considering what they charged for tickets to this ridiculous party, they could afford a decent spread.

"What would you like?" he asked, amused by the hungry greed she made no effort to conceal.

"Some of everything," she answered promptly. "Let's start with the desserts."

He laughed in genuine amusement, amazed that he still remembered how. "Not worried about calories?"

"Oh, no," she assured blithely. "I find plenty of ways to burn them off."

He lifted an eyebrow, wondering if she meant that to sound as suggestive as it did. "Burn them off, how?" he probed, handing her a china plate. "Busy nights?"

She helped herself to a huge slice of fudge cake. "Very." Taking a deep breath, she glanced at him, her expression determinedly frank. "I work as a waitress and dishwasher. Correction. I *worked* as a waitress and dishwasher. I'm not even that anymore."

Which explained the hands. As for his innuendo, she hadn't picked up on that at all. Surely she wasn't so naive. He frowned. Or was she? What if she were—he blanched—a virgin? Hell, he couldn't handle that. Virgins expected permanency. Commitment. Romance. Virgins expected forever. He needed someone experienced. Someone who knew what she was getting into. Someone who wouldn't balk when it came time to perform her marital duties and would then have the gumption to admit as much to Judge Graydon.

Someone who'd walk away from him without a backward glance.

"How old are you, anyway?" he asked suspiciously.

"Twenty-six."

He couldn't hide his relief. Twenty-six. That was encouraging. There couldn't be many twenty-six-year-old virgins left in the world. Still... There was something about her. Something pure and innocent and fresh that made him feel as skittish as a stallion with his first mare. "You ever slept with a man?" he demanded bluntly.

She didn't appear anywhere near as stunned as the diners who'd overheard his question. She tilted her head to one side and blinked up at him. "Should I have?"

"Yes. Without question."

"Oh." She slipped a raspberry tart onto her plate. "Well, if it helps any, I've been engaged three times."

His hands tightened on his plate. Damnation. Three times. Three men. Three engagements worth of opportunity to lure his little elf into someone else's bed. He should feel relieved. Instead he felt murderous. "Three times, huh?"

"Yes."

She looked at him and he read the truth in her eyes. Three men had had her within their grasp and not held on. Were they blind, stupid, or just crazy? He took her plate out of her hands and jerked his head toward an open doorway. "Come on. Let's find someplace private to talk. I want to get this settled."

She cast a wistful glance toward the desserts they'd missed and then accompanied him out a set of French doors and into the garden. The November desert was unseasonably warm, the evening chill barely penetrating. Imported trees and shrubbery glittered with fairy lights, a full moon splashing the pathways with interesting patterns of illumination and shadow. Tables and benches were recessed into little nooks and, wandering deeper into the garden, Jake found an empty one.

"Tell me why you want to marry," he began peremptorily, setting their plates on the table.

She sat, her gown shimmering softly in the subdued starlight, her hair and eyes burnished with silver. "I was afraid you were going to ask that." She shot him a hopeful glance, nibbling at a morsel of rum cake. "I don't suppose you'd care to go first?"

"Okay," he consented, shoving his plate to one side. "It's quite simple. I have an inheritance at stake. I either marry or I lose it." His voice deepened, grew cool and stark. "And just so you know, I don't intend to lose it."

She lowered her fork and stared at him in astonished delight. "That's wonderful."

He leaned across the table, pinning her with a look of cold displeasure. "I'm about to lose my inheritance and you think it's wonderful?"

"No, no. You don't understand."

"Then explain it so I will."

"I have an inheritance, too. And the only way I can keep it, is if I marry." She peeked up at him. "Quite a coincidence, don't you think?"

He lifted an eyebrow, thinking it a little too convenient a coincidence. "Then why do you need a permanent marriage?" he asked skeptically.

"I told you. It doesn't have to be permanent. It's just..." She hesitated, as though choosing her words carefully—something he suspected she didn't often bother with. "You see, there's this woman. Mrs. Marsh. She wants my inheritance and she'll do whatever it takes to get it away from me." She frowned, her expression turning fierce. "She's already scared off three fiancés.

That's why I need someone strong, someone who'll help me fight her.''

That explained a lot. Her previous fiancés sounded like total bastards, making promises they had no intention of keeping. All so they could entice her into their beds, he didn't doubt. ''I don't scare easy,'' Jake commented. ''And I've never yet failed to keep my word.''

She grinned. ''I hoped you'd say that. Which leaves only one problem.''

Of course. While he'd been distracted by the more pleasurable aspects of having her as his wife, she'd been baiting her trap. A trap he'd almost fallen into. When would he learn? Nothing ever came without a price. ''What's your problem?'' he asked grimly.

''You want a brief marriage. But I don't know how long it will take to get rid of Mrs. Marsh, to convince her that she can't take my inheritance away from me.''

''I don't understand. Once you're married—''

''The inheritance is mine. Legally. But if she finds out it's only a temporary marriage, she'll never give up. She'll try to get her hands on it after we divorce. She'll argue that the marriage was just a ruse.''

He shrugged. ''Then we'll have to make sure she doesn't learn about the divorce.''

Wynne nibbled on her lower lip. ''If she does, I guess I could find myself another husband.''

Jake stilled, fighting the surge of displeasure her comment stirred. He had no right to feel that way. Once she'd fulfilled her marital duty, it wasn't any of his business what Wynne chose to do. He'd help get rid of this Marsh woman for now. Later could take care of itself. He hesitated, aware their deal wasn't the least equitable. She still had the chance to find someone else, someone who'd stick around longer, who could guarantee Mrs. Marsh would never be a problem.

"I'm not right for you," he said in a low voice. He stood, pulling her to her feet. "Go back to the ballroom and take another look around. Maybe you'll find the perfect man, a permanent sort of man."

She shook her head and smiled. "I've already found the perfect man."

He'd give her one final chance to escape. If she stayed, she'd seal her own fate. It would be out of his hands and he could take her with a clear conscience. "Run away, little elf," he insisted curtly. "Go now, while you still can. You don't want me for your husband. I'll only hurt you."

"You could never hurt me," she said, lifting her face to his.

"You don't think so?" His hands closed on the narrow bones of her shoulders and he tugged her into his arms. "Why don't we find out?"

And unable to resist any longer, he took her mouth with his.

CHAPTER TWO

WYNNE STOOD CLASPED in Jake's arms, reveling in the most incredible kiss she'd ever received. He'd meant for it to be ruthless; she'd known from the grim set of his jaw and the hard grasp of his hands. He'd meant to scare her off. But somewhere between the time he'd pulled her close and the time he'd kissed her, his intentions must have changed.

He groaned, his mouth moving over hers with gentle warmth, probing, sampling, tasting at will. It was as though he were indulging in a leisurely exploration, stirring her in ways that emptied every thought from her head save one—to experience more. He must have sensed her total capitulation, for his touch grew more assured, firmer, coaxing a response unlike any she'd known before.

Did he suspect how thoroughly shaken she was by his kiss, how new and wonderful she found it? He'd been so concerned about her level of sexual expertise earlier, so appalled that she might still be a virgin. And yet, his kiss seemed to take that possibility into consideration, easing from the lightest of caresses to a more potent, heady embrace.

She stood on tiptoe, pressing closer, determined to enjoy every aspect of this unexpected treat. In response, he molded her against him, his body hard, his arousal blatant. His hands swept over her with unmistakable skill, as though committing each curve to memory. His touch burned, igniting a reaction that grew more intense

31

by the moment. She trembled uncontrollably, desire overriding every other thought and emotion.

"Jake, please!"

The cry escaped before she could prevent it. For a crazed instant she thought he'd tumble them into the bushes and take her right then and there. Instead he tensed and pushed her away, cool air replacing the unbearable heat of seconds ago. She fought him, refusing to leave the protective warmth of his arms.

"We can't take this any further, Wynne," he murmured close to her ear. "This isn't what I'd planned."

She clung to him, shivering, struggling to regain her equilibrium. "What did you plan?"

"To drive you off." His response was stark, yet painfully honest.

"Oh." She snuggled deeper into his arms, burying her face in the curve of his shoulder. She fit as though made for him. "You didn't succeed."

"I can see that," he said with a soft laugh. "Does this mean we're committed?"

She forced herself to consider his question rationally, to control the emotional upheaval clouding her mind. Her mouth curved in a wry smile. It was an impossible task. How could she think when all she wanted was to lose herself in his embrace? She'd never fallen in love before, certainly not with a man she'd only known for a few brief hours. She didn't have a clue how to separate reason from sentiment.

"Wynne?" Tension rippled through him and his arms tightened around her. "Have you changed your mind?"

She shook her head. "No. I haven't changed my mind." Pulling back, she looked up at him. "You said 'committed.' Is that a proposal, by any chance?"

He hesitated. "It's a proposition for a temporary marriage."

She wouldn't get any more from him than that. At least, not yet. Not that it mattered. She'd have plenty of time to prove he needed her on a permanent basis. After all, who knew how long it would take to convince Mrs. Marsh that their marriage was real? A week, a month, six months? Those six months could become six years, she was certain of it. And six years could become sixty.

"In that case, I accept," she agreed. "Though I'll be happy to stick around longer if you want."

"I won't." Steel had crept into his voice. "Don't think you can alter my decision about this, Wynne. It won't happen. This marriage is a temporary arrangement."

"Whatever you say." She sighed, sliding her fingers through his crisp, dark hair. "Would you kiss me again? I rather liked it. It was nice."

He frowned. "Nice, huh? Remind me not to ask you for a reference."

Color tinted her cheeks. "Well... I liked kissing you enough to want it to go on for the rest of the night."

"It can."

If he meant to alarm her with his bluntness, he failed. Miserably. She stared in wonder, lifting her mouth to his. "Really? All night?"

He set her from him, his fierce gaze telling her all too clearly how much of a temptation he found her—a temptation he intended to resist. "All we have to do is get this farce of a wedding over with. I have a room at the Grand Hotel and we'll go there the minute we're married. Once that's out of the way, we can make this night last as long as you'd like."

Her smile grew luminous. "That's just perfect. I'm staying at the Grand, too."

"Listen to me, Wynne...." His tone cut through her euphoria, sounding deadly serious. "There's one or two details we haven't agreed on."

"Is that all?" she teased in an effort to hide her nervousness. "Just one or two?"

"When we get to the Grand..." He hesitated as though searching for words, then stated flatly, "I expect to consummate the marriage. If you're not certain you can handle that, now's the time to back out."

"I won't back out," she replied instantly. Why would she? He was perfect. He was everything she'd always wanted in a man. She'd discovered her knight in shining armor, just as she'd known she would. No. Without a doubt, she'd find joy in this marriage and with this man, no matter how long their time together might last. An impish smile played about her mouth. Of course, she intended it to last a bit longer than he did. "That's one detail taken care of. What else is there?"

"I have a prenuptial agreement I want you to sign."

She shrugged. "No problem. Give me a pen and I'll sign it."

His mouth tightened. "You won't sign a damned thing until you've read it."

"Fine, I'll read it. Why? What does it say?"

"That when we divorce, my inheritance stays with me." His gaze met hers, his eyes direct and unflinching in their regard. "All of it."

"Well, of course. That's the whole point of the marriage, right?"

He gathered her hands in his. "It occurred to me that you might be marrying for more than just an inheritance."

She stared down at their joined hands. Hers were engulfed in his, and she frowned at how red and chapped her skin remained despite all the moisturizer she'd used. Did he despise the roughness? she couldn't help but wonder. She'd always thought it a small price to pay when balanced against all she stood to gain.

"I told you why I need a husband," she said, not quite certain what he was implying. "What more could there be?"

"Maybe you're tired of working so hard to make ends meet and are looking for someone to help ease your burden." It was the gentlest of accusations and carefully phrased—quite out of character for such a blunt, cut-to-the-chase type man.

"I see," she murmured. "You think because I work hard, I'm unhappy."

He shook his head. "Not unhappy. Just anxious to start a new life. Marriage can look damned appealing if it means escaping a lifetime of drudgery."

She smiled in relief. "I can understand why you might think that. And you're right. I do work hard to make ends meet." In fact, if he knew the whole truth he'd consider her situation quite desperate. No money. No job. No place to live. But that was only a temporary condition.

"Is that why you're marrying, to escape your current life?"

"No," she stated without hesitation. "Some people might see marriage as a way out. But I'm not one of them. I have my health. I've never been afraid of hard work. And when things go wrong, I do whatever it takes to right my situation. Marriage only ensures I hold onto my inheritance."

She'd deal with the rest of her troubles when the time came—when her marriage ended. *If* her marriage ended, she couldn't prevent the wistful thought.

"That's it? You're marrying in order to gain control of your inheritance. No strings attached?"

"I don't need your money," she said with absolute sincerity. "Or whatever else your inheritance might be. I just need you. If you'll give me the paper and a pen, I'll be happy to sign the agreement."

He studied her for a long moment, then nodded. "That's the last of my conditions. This would be a good time to name any you might have."

"All I want is your help fighting Mrs. Marsh," she said. "Once we're married, I expect you to stick by me."

A sardonic smile edged his mouth. "You have my unconditional support for the length of our marriage. Guaranteed."

She eyed him keenly. "Even if that isn't as short a time as you'd prefer?"

He didn't like the implication, but to her relief, he didn't argue. "Yes."

"I hope you mean that."

"You doubt my word?" he asked ominously.

She gave an awkward shrug. "It's not that. It's just that none of my former fiancés lived up to their promises. Mrs. Marsh scared them all off."

"I'm not those other men," he snapped. "I keep my word."

She prayed he'd still feel that way once he knew the complete truth. But somehow she doubted it. "Do we have a deal, then?"

"We do."

She smiled up at him, daring to tease. "Shall we seal it with another kiss?"

His eyes glittered dangerously. "Not wise, elf."

"Maybe not. But it is enjoyable."

He shook his head. "I prefer we do this by the book. First we'll take care of the prenuptial agreement. Then we'll have a wedding."

"And the kiss?"

Passion marked his expression, burning in the fevered gold of his eyes. "Once we're back at the hotel and in the privacy of our own room, you can have as many as you want."

As many as she wanted... The thought fired her imagination. It seemed too good to be true. Soon she'd be married to Jake, she'd make love to him. Excitement stirred, and with that excitement came a fragile hope that their relationship would be blessed, that she could fill the emptiness he carried like a leaden weight and vanquish his demons. That a special joy would come from their joining, a joy unlike any they'd known before.

He needs me, she repeated silently. *And I need him.*

"Sit down and take a look at these papers," he requested, spreading them out on the table.

She resumed her seat and tilted the documents so the glow from a nearby lantern fell across them. To her relief, the agreement appeared simple and straightforward. Jake stood over her, insisting she read every word. Once done, she signed without a qualm, then glanced up at him. "What's next?"

"We have to fill out an application before we can marry. There's a county clerk stationed in the library with the necessary documentation."

Wynne smiled. "Which means all we have to do is find the library."

Footmen were quick to direct them and they discovered the county clerk seated behind a massive oak desk processing marriage applications. Her name tag read, Dora Scott, and she'd propped a sign next to her that announced, "For faster service, feed me hors d'oeuvres."

"Cute," Jake murmured, amused. He gestured for a footman and inclined his head toward the sign. "Bring a tray of your best."

Dora overheard and grinned. "I appreciate that. You two in a hurry, or just kindhearted?"

Jake propped a hip on the desk. "No one has ever accused me of being kindhearted."

"Which leaves...in a hurry," the clerk said with a laugh. "Well, it just so happens you've caught me during a lull. Let's see what I can do." With a speed that left Wynne breathless, Dora whipped through the formalities. Completing the paperwork, she explained each in detail and handed them a pretty blue-and-white envelope. "Give these forms to whomever you choose to officiate the ceremony. The gold sealed certificate is a souvenir, for decoration only. You can frame it, hang it on your wall or throw darts at it for all I care. But it's not a legal document, so don't go trying to palm it off as one."

"No problem," Jake said. "Thanks for your help."

"My pleasure. Just do me one favor."

"Sure."

The clerk held him with a piercing gaze. "Be happy. That's all I ask. Now go on and get out of here. I've got another couple waiting and by the look of the hors d'oeuvres he's carrying they're in an even bigger hurry than you two."

Documents in hand, Jake and Wynne crossed to the salons set aside for the wedding ceremonies. "It seems we have a choice," she murmured. "Religious, civil..."

"Or anything in between," Jake finished for her, his voice unexpectedly harsh. "Which do you prefer?"

She glanced at him, about to answer, then caught her breath in dismay. He stood unmoving, his jaw set in rigid lines, his shoulders tensed as though in anticipation of a blow. He dreaded this next part, she realized in dismay. She could see it in the turbulent glitter of his eyes and the rigid line of his mouth. Of all that had gone before, *this* would be the most difficult for him. Why? she couldn't help but wonder. What painful memories lay beneath that stoic expression?

Tears of sympathy gathered in her eyes and she blinked to clear them before he noticed. He wouldn't appreciate her compassion. In fact, it might very well drive him away. If she wanted to help, she'd get this next part over with as quickly as possible. She sighed. All her life she'd dreamt of walking down the aisle of her hometown church. At the very least she'd hoped for a quiet, religious service, its simplicity both moving and memorable. Now she knew she'd have neither. It would be asking too much.

"Why don't we have a civil ceremony," she suggested gently.

Jake nodded in agreement, relief easing the tension consuming him. He led the way into the appropriate salon, hesitating once inside the room. A frown creased his brow. She looked around, wondering what had caused his displeasure. The room was decorated in an elegant, if rather formal fashion, a pale blue silk couch and chairs grouped at one side of the room with small dried flower arrangements gracing the walnut end tables. At the opposite side a podium stood in front of drawn drapes, a justice of the peace officiating an unpretentious ceremony.

"Is there something wrong?" she whispered.

His frown deepened. "Let's take a look at the other rooms." He didn't wait for her response, but turned and led the way to the next salon.

Wynne stepped through the open doorway of this room and caught her breath in delight, feeling as if she'd just escaped from the bleakness of a wintery landscape into the comforting warmth of a summer evening.

Subdued lighting flickered across a vaulted ceiling trimmed in cypress wood, a bank of windows stretching across one full wall of the room. Brass containers lined the base of the windows, overflowing with fresh flowers, their heady scent filling the air. And in the middle stood the altar. Vivaldi played softly in the background like a benediction, and in that moment she knew. She wanted to be married here. It was the perfect place for a perfect wedding.

"We could look at the other rooms," she offered reluctantly. "See what other choices are available."

Jake shook her head. "No need. This will do."

Once again they'd arrived during a lull and the elderly minister motioned for them to approach the altar. She could see their reflection in the windows, pale and ghostly. And she could see beyond the glass, to a midnight sky lit by the moon and stars. Far below, the fairy lights twinkled among the trees and shrubs.

"It's like standing between heaven and earth," she whispered, tucking her hand into the crook of Jake's arm.

The minister smiled at her comment. "It is, isn't it? I think this is my favorite room for just that reason. Do you wish to be married?" he asked.

"Yes, please," Wynne said, as Jake handed over the necessary papers.

"Before we start I'm required to ask that you give careful consideration to what you're about to do," the minister began, his gentle blue eyes turning somber. "Marriage is a serious commitment, not to be entered into lightly. So I ask that you face each other and look carefully at your partner. Make sure that your choice is the right one."

Wynne turned and stared into Jake's eyes. They had darkened in color to a deep, rich shade of honey, all emotion held carefully in check. He was such a bewildering contradiction, she thought. He confronted the world with uncompromising aggression, with a fierceness that defied resistance. Even his eyes were those of a wild animal, spirited and untamed and predatory. And yet his face suggested an austere nature, his expression stern and unapproachable, giving even the most combative personalities pause. He made his home in darkness and shadow, and she wondered if some painful incident in his past had forced him to turn his back on the light of human warmth.

Or was it that he wanted people to think the worst? came the stunning thought. Not that she ever could.

She offered a reassuring smile. He might intimidate some, but she'd sensed the goodness he worked so hard to conceal. From the moment she'd first seen him, she'd sensed his strength of character, his innate decency and had known he'd make the perfect husband. She'd been so worried that the man she selected would be getting the raw end of the deal, that she would be receiving far more. But with Jake there was no cause for concern. She could give him his dream—his inheritance. Better yet, she could give him what he lacked most in life...love.

She glanced toward the minister. Was she certain of her choice? Without question. The answer was *yes*.

Jake stared at the woman clinging to his arm and then at the minister, dread balling in the pit of his stomach. Was he certain of his choice? Without question. The answer was *no*.

He found Wynne a bewildering contradiction—soft and sweet, and yet surprisingly sensuous. Her smile alone made him lose every thought in his head. She was a glorious mix of fire and innocence—a volatile combination. He frowned, realizing he hadn't been so rattled by a woman since adolescence. That alone should make him wary.

But what disturbed him the most were her eyes. A vivid green, they appeared as open and compelling as a child's. They shone with an inner purity his touch would surely corrupt. Worse, they held a shrewdness that swept past all barriers, that stripped bare the blackness of his soul. He didn't understand it. If she saw him so clearly, why did she stay? He glanced at her again, stared into those huge, beautiful eyes, and what he saw made his chest tighten.

She may have agreed to temporary, but her eyes promised forever.

"Have you reached a decision?" the minister asked.

Jake started to answer, to end the farce before it went any further, but then realized he wasn't the one being addressed. Apparently the minister didn't doubt that Wynne would make an acceptable bride. No. His concern was whether the bride would regret saddling herself with such an unlikely husband. It shouldn't surprise him.

"Please begin the ceremony," Wynne said, perfectly calm and collected. Perfectly willing.

For an instant, Jake wavered between making the noble choice by backing out...or remaining silent and letting her pay the ultimate price for her folly by marrying her. He gritted his teeth, torn. How could he allow her to commit such an ill-advised act? This marriage wouldn't be fair to her. She wouldn't get anything out of it—except a wealth of heartache. And he'd caused enough heartache without inflicting anymore.

What about the inheritance? a relentless voice questioned. If he didn't marry Wynne, his chances of finding another bride before the deadline were next to nil. Besides, he wanted her. He wanted her in his bed and in his home. In that moment, he wanted her almost as much as he did his inheritance.

And then it was too late, the choice taken from him.

"I do," he heard her say.

She smiled up at him as she said it, her eyes shining, trapping him in a pool of glorious green sunshine. He stared back, his own responses to the minister barely registering.

"Before I pronounce you man and wife, would you care to exchange rings? We have them on hand," the minister offered, peering at them from over his spectacles. "They're tokens, really. Just something to use until you're able to replace them with the genuine article."

"That isn't necessary," Jake replied, digging into his pocket and pulling out a simple gold band. He'd picked an average-size ring, but to his amusement, it proved far too large, forcing Wynne to make a fist in order to keep it on. Not that it seemed to bother her.

"It's beautiful," she whispered. "I'll treasure it forever."

"You'll treasure it for the *brief* length of our marriage," he retorted in a hard voice.

But she shook her head, leveling him with another of those bewitching smiles as sensuous as it was innocent. "No. I'll treasure this ring for the rest of my life because it's given me everything I've always wanted." Then her brow wrinkled in concern. "But what about you? Where's your ring?"

"I don't need one." Their marriage was a temporary measure, not worthy of a ring to symbolize the event.

Understanding dawned in her eyes and with that understanding came a terrible sadness, one that totally devastated his defenses.

And as the minister pronounced them husband and wife, Jake realized he was in deep, deep trouble.

Wynne knelt on the carpet, eyeing the hotel door in disgust. For the tenth time she stabbed the card into the locking mechanism and for the tenth time a red button flashed its rejection.

"Whatever happened to keys?" she muttered. "I liked keys. And keys liked me. At least they unlocked the—" The door opened and she practically tumbled into the room.

Laura stood there, dressed in a nightgown and robe. "Oh, thank goodness! I thought I heard you. I was getting worried," she exclaimed, then frowned in concern. "What were you doing on the floor?"

"I was trying to get this stupid thing to work," Wynne said, holding up the card key as she struggled to her feet.

Laura froze, staring at Wynne's hand. "You're wearing a ring! You did it, didn't you? You're married."

"Yes, I'm married," Wynne said with a smile, wriggling her fingers so the light flickered across her wedding band. It slid off her knuckle and she hastened to push it back in place. "Oh, Laura, I'm so glad you came with me. Now I can tell you all about him. He's wonderful. He's everything I'd hoped."

Laura grinned, tears leaping to her eyes. "I'm so relieved. I've spent the night worrying that some fast-talking rat would take advantage of you. Who is he? What does he do? How old is he?"

Wynne stared at her blankly. "I . . . I'm not sure. But, his name is Jake . . . Jake . . . Good grief. Considering we're married, you'd think I'd remember his last name," she muttered. "Oh, never mind. His name's not all that important. It's Jake something-or-other."

Laura's tears evaporated, along with her smile. "Jake something-or-other? You can't remember your own husband's name and you don't think that's important?" she questioned ominously.

"No. What *is* important is that he's perfect. Absolutely perfect. And he's the sweetest man in the world." She hesitated. "Well . . . To be honest, I suppose he isn't all that sweet. No, sweet's the wrong word."

Laura groaned. "What's the right word?"

"Tough. Strong." Wynne smiled cheerfully. "Hard as nails would be a pretty accurate description. Mrs. Marsh doesn't stand a chance against him."

"Hard as nails, huh? That's good. I guess," Laura said with a marked lack of enthusiasm. "Where is he from?"

Wynne shrugged. "I never thought to ask. Someplace further down south, I think. He has an accent—or rather a drawl."

"I don't believe this! You don't remember his name, never bothered to ask where he's from, or what he does for a living. Nor do you know how old he is. Is it just me or is there something wrong with this picture?" She tightened the belt of her bathrobe and glared at Wynne. "What, precisely, *do* you know about this man? Why does he need a wife?"

Wynne smiled in relief. "Now that one I can answer. He needs a wife in order to keep his inheritance."

"And what's his inheritance?"

"I...I don't know. Does it matter?"

"Of course it matters! What if—" Laura paused, her eyes narrowing. "There's something you're not telling me. What is it?"

Wynne peeked at her friend from beneath her lashes. "I'd really rather not say."

"I'd really rather you did." Laura folded her arms across her chest. "Please. Tell me. What are you hiding?"

"Just wait until you meet him. You'll think he's perfect, too," Wynne hastened to assure. "And he's a good man, though I suspect he wouldn't agree."

"He wouldn't agree? Wynne! What sort of person did you marry? Tough, hard, strong. He sounds like some sort of brute. And you still haven't answered my question. What have you left out?"

Wynne cleared her throat. "Not much. And he's not a brute! He's the kind of man who can take care of Mrs. Marsh. He's more than a match for her, even if he only wants a temporary marriage." She could see this latest piece of news didn't go over well.

Laura looked stunned. "A temporary marriage? You spent all your money on a temporary marriage? I can't believe this! What happens when it ends? You'll be right back where you started. No job. No money. No place to live. How will that help? Mrs. Marsh still wins and you'll have gone through all this for nothing."

"Jake won't let that happen," Wynne insisted stubbornly. "He says he isn't interested in a permanent relationship, but I think he'll change his mind."

"You're willing to gamble everything on a bunch of maybes? You're willing to risk losing—"

"I won't lose a thing," Wynne interrupted, her voice sharper than she'd intended. She took a deep breath, fighting for composure. "Please, Laura. Let's not argue. This is my wedding night, and I'm so happy. Wait until you meet him. You'll see what I mean. You'll understand why I'm so certain he's the right man."

"You're spending the night with him?" Laura demanded apprehensively.

Wynne nodded. "He's asked me to and I've agreed. I came by to pick up my overnight bag and check on you. Is everything all right?"

"Oh, everything's fine here," Laura claimed. "Blissfully quiet. But what about you? Maybe you should—"

Wynne cut her off. "Maybe I should get my bag and join my husband," she said with gentle finality.

Laura raised her hands in surrender. "Okay. I give up. It's your life to live as you see fit."

"Don't be angry," Wynne pleaded. "You're my best friend. Try to be happy for me. I've been dreaming of this moment all my life. I have an incredible husband and a whole new life ahead of me."

"Right. Besides, look at the bright side," Laura said dryly. "If things don't work out, you have an automatic escape clause."

"Oh, I won't need it," Wynne claimed, flashing an impish smile. "And if I have anything to say about it, neither will Jake."

CHAPTER THREE

JAKE STOOD IN FRONT of the hotel window looking out at a starlit night, lost in the darkness of his thoughts. Would Wynne come? he wondered. Or would she have second thoughts about the wisdom of their marriage and run? He didn't want to care one way or the other. But he did. His future hung in the balance, the choices made by a pint-size elf the determining factor. He clenched his hands, jamming them into the pockets of his robe. Damn. He'd never felt so out-of-control in his life.

And he didn't like the feeling.

A knock sounded then—not a soft, tentative rap, but a rapid, eager tattoo. Suppressing a smile of satisfaction, he strode to the door, flinging it open.

Wynne stood on the threshold, her green eyes peeping at him from beneath wispy white bangs. "Hi," she said.

He lounged in the doorway, his tension fading beneath the sunny warmth of her smile. "Hi, yourself."

She tilted her head to one side. "Were you afraid I wouldn't show up?" she asked gently.

Was he so transparent? "The thought crossed my mind." He forced out the admission, and stepped aside so she could enter.

"You'll find I'm really quite trustworthy," she assured, glancing around the suite with interest. "But since you don't know me very well, I can understand your not realizing that."

"Thanks for filling me in," he retorted dryly, taking her bag.

Her gaze settled on him, the passion and vitality in that one look as powerful as a physical blow. It never ceased to amaze him how different she was from all the other women he'd known. How had so much zeal been bundled into such a tiny package?

"You've showered," she said, stating the obvious. "Would you mind if I did, too?"

"Be my guest. There's another of these hotel robes hanging on the door. Feel free to use it."

"Thanks, but I have a nightgown." She gestured toward the case he held. "If you wouldn't mind?"

"I don't mind." He tossed the bag to her. "But you won't need it. Not for long."

A hectic flush chased across her cheekbones and Jake regretted the crassness of his remark. There were times he felt like the proverbial bull in the china shop—and this was one of them. She gave a shrug that showed amazing sangfroid considering her obvious embarrassment, and crossed to the bathroom.

She seemed so young and fragile from the back, her shoulders fine-boned, the graceful sweep of her neck highlighted by the short pixieish cut of her hair. He'd never realized the nape of a woman's neck could look so vulnerable. A sudden urge to protect her gripped him. But then he realized the only protection she needed was from her husband.

She hesitated at the doorway to the bathroom and glanced over her shoulder. "Oh, I meant to ask when I first arrived," she said unexpectedly. "What's your...*our* last name? I'm afraid I've forgotten."

His mouth tightened. "Hondo," he replied, then stated with cool deliberation, "it was my mother's name."

He couldn't tell whether she'd picked up on the significance of his comment or whether she deliberately feigned ignorance. Or didn't it matter to her? He shook his head, unwilling to believe she found his parentage inconsequential. The people of Chesterfield considered it of critical importance.

"Hondo," she repeated. A tiny smile played around her mouth and his gut clenched at the guileless sensuality. "Wynne Hondo," she said, as though tasting the words. Then she laughed aloud. "It doesn't fit me half as well as it does you. But maybe it will in time."

She shouldered her overnight bag and disappeared into the bathroom, leaving him to mull over what she'd meant by "in time." It had better mean damned short and not a second longer. The splash of the shower interrupted his thoughts and he became instantly aware that every sound she made reverberated through the thin walls.

He could hear the material of her gown rustle as she removed it and pictured her stripping—baring soft, pearly skin. He knew the minute she stepped beneath the steamy spray, her murmur of pleasure as seductive as a siren's song. It took every ounce of willpower not to thrust open the door and join her. Would she complain... or would she welcome him? He reached for the knob, determined to find out.

She'd be slippery with soap, wet and sleek. If he found her willing, he'd take her in his arms and make her his wife in fact as well as name. But before he could follow through, the water stopped and he hesitated, annoyed that the choice had been taken from him. He released the knob and stepped back and after a few short moments she emerged from the bathroom.

He froze at the sight of her, unable to draw breath, feeling like someone had smashed an iron fist into his chest. He seesawed on the edge of control, rock-hard with desire, passion driving him to the point of no return. Only one thing kept him from plunging over the edge and taking what he wanted....

Wynne's nightgown.

His wife stood uncertainly in the doorway, enveloped in whisper-thin cotton. The nightgown floated around her like mist, clinging for a moment as it caressed the pure, graceful curves of her body before swirling away. But one detail stopped him dead in his tracks... the damned thing was white. Stark white. Snow white. Unadulterated, unsullied, virginal white, the color as untainted as the woman who wore it. Three men, he struggled to remind himself. She'd said three men. He shook his head in disbelief. It couldn't be. It wasn't possible.

Because once they'd touched her, how the hell could they have walked away?

She moved into the room. Light from the bedside table threw her body into silhouette, almost bringing him to his knees. It was the most erotic sight he'd ever beheld, crippling in its impact. For such a little thing, her figure was all woman. She had a narrow waist that flared into sweetly rounded hips, her backside exhibiting just the right amount of curve. Her breasts shifted beneath her nightgown, the nipples dark shadows that pearled before his eyes. With a muttered exclamation, he forced his attention upward and away from temptation.

She stood quietly, staring at him, her eyes huge and wary, her hair tousled and damp from her shower. He didn't say a word, but simply held out his hand. After a momentary hesitation, she slipped her fingers into his.

"I see why you wanted to wear this instead of a robe," he said, his voice husky with need. "It's very provocative."

"Really?" She glanced down, her brows drawn together. "I always thought it rather modest."

He chuckled. "Your idea of modest must differ from mine." He reached for her, running his index finger along the curve of her breast, pausing at the peak to draw lazy circles around the rigid tip.

Her head jerked upward and she stared at him, her eyes enormous, the green turning as dark as a shadow-draped forest. She moistened her lips. "Could we turn off the lights?" she requested anxiously.

"The lights stay on. I want to see you when we make love."

She didn't argue, but some of the color ebbed from her face. "I didn't expect to feel this nervous," she confessed. "But I can't seem to stop shaking. Are you sure we can't turn off the lights? Just this once?"

His mouth tightened and he left her for a moment, flicking the switch on the bedside lamp. The room plunged into darkness, relieved only by the faint illumination from a fast sinking moon. "Better?"

"Much, thank you." She drifted across the room, the conspicuous white of her nightgown marking her progress. "Should I... should I get into bed?"

He bit back a caustic comeback, aware that something was out of kilter, but too hard-ridden by desire to analyze what it might be. "Sure. Get into bed if it makes you more comfortable."

"Actually I'm thirsty," she said, veering toward the bathroom. "I think I'd like some—"

He blocked her path, catching her off guard. She looked at him, startled, and her breath came swift and uneven. He didn't hesitate, but took her mouth in a demanding kiss. He felt, rather than heard, her small murmur of protest. She stiffened, not quite fighting him, but not responding as she had at the Montagues'.

He lifted his head and stared down at her. "Relax," he murmured, stroking his thumb along the tender curve of her cheek. "You want this as much as I do."

"I thought I did," she said, a tiny catch robbing the certainty from her voice. "I seem to be having second thoughts."

"You won't for long."

His mouth dropped over hers once again and he molded her closer, exploring the shapely curves beneath the thin cotton nightgown. If he'd had any lingering qualms about taking advantage of her, they vanished, dissolving beneath his desperate need to possess the woman in his arms. She belonged to him now, and he meant to take what was his.

He released the buttons fastening the bodice of her nightgown and swept the material from her shoulders, baring her to his intent gaze. Moonlight lanced across the paleness of her skin, carving tempting shadows between her gently rounded breasts. He groaned, lowering his mouth to taste her perfection.

She seemed to shudder, though she didn't make a sound, merely lifted a hand to brush the hair from his brow. The muted gleam of her wedding band distracted him and he pulled back, looking at her, seeing her clearly for the first time that night.

And what he saw stopped him cold.

A solitary tear traced a path down the waxen curve of her cheek, and he took a quick step back, disgusted by what he'd been about to do. And yet, despite that disgust, every instinct he possessed railed at him to finish what he'd started, to put his mark on her in the most basic way possible. He'd never considered himself noble or honorable or decent. Tonight confirmed that beyond any doubt. But looking into Wynne's wide, unflinching eyes, seeing her acceptance of such an untenable situation very nearly unmanned him.

What the hell had he done, marrying her like this?

He took another step back and then another and another until he'd put as much room between them as he could. "Get in the bed," he whispered harshly.

Still she didn't speak, merely drew her nightgown back in place and obeyed. She clambered onto the mattress, and in that moment, he knew. He couldn't touch her, couldn't risk hurting her. Not now. Not even if it meant losing the inheritance he'd fought so hard to win.

He forced himself to turn his back on her, staring instead at the desert skirting the hotel, feeling oddly at one with the bleak beauty. Slowly the serenity of the landscape crept into his soul, calming him, and he gained a small measure of control. Only the strongest and most determined survived in such an arid section of the country—just as only through sheer strength and determination had he survived the aridness of his youth. But his survival had never been at anyone's expense but his own.

Until now.

"Jake...?"

He didn't turn around. "Go to sleep, elf. We'll talk in the morning."

He heard the rustle of sheets as she left the bed and approached, felt her icy hand slip across his bicep. "Have I done something wrong?" she questioned quietly.

His laugh rang out, cold and humorless. "Yeah. You did something wrong. You married me."

"No," she protested. "Marrying you was the smartest thing I ever did."

He spun around, grabbing her shoulders. "Don't you get it? Don't you realize what happened here tonight? I almost... I almost...." He couldn't speak the words, couldn't admit he'd nearly committed such a vile act.

"Don't say it," she urged, pressing her fingertips to his mouth. "You did nothing wrong. I'm your wife, remember? You could never hurt me."

"If that's what you really believe, then you're setting yourself up for a mighty big fall." He stepped away, warning, "It's not wise to stand this close, not the way I'm feeling right now. Wife or not, it's clear I can't be trusted."

She stood her ground. "Don't be ridiculous. I'd trust you with my life. Please come to bed with me, Jake. I don't want to sleep alone on our wedding night."

He shook his head. "You don't know what you're asking."

"No, I don't suppose I do. Come, anyway." She tilted her head to one side and a smile trembled at the corners of her mouth, erasing all vestige of her earlier tears. "I promise I won't take advantage of you."

Not bothering to argue further, he swept her into his arms and carried her to the bed. Tucking her carefully beneath the covers, he started to return to his stance by the window, but found it impossible to leave her side. Instead he stripped off his robe and joined her between the sheets. More than anything he wanted to pull her into his arms. But that would be begging for trouble. He'd narrowly escaped their last encounter with his sanity intact. He'd never escape this one if he gave in and held her again.

"Jake?"

"I'm right here," he murmured gently. "Try to get some sleep."

"What about your requirement—that we consummate the marriage tonight?"

"Forget it," he said, slinging an arm across his eyes. "It was an unreasonable demand."

"If you say so. But if you change your mind..."

"I won't."

Silence reigned for a moment or two, then, "Jake?"

"What is it?"

"I really am glad I married you."

He swallowed the thickness blocking his throat. "Me, too, elf. Me, too."

Jake awoke in that timeless moment between the black of night and the first light of dawn, not quite certain what had disturbed him. A whispery sigh drifted from the other side of the mattress and he turned his head. Wynne lay facing him, sound asleep, and in that instant reality came crashing down. He was married—a condition he'd sworn he'd avoid—and this slip of a woman was his wife. He gritted his teeth, calling himself every kind of a fool. What had he been thinking, marrying someone so clearly out of her element? He must have lost his mind.

She murmured a name—his name, perhaps—and he propped himself on one elbow, studying her. She'd kicked off her covers during the night and her nightgown had ridden up, hugging her slender hips. She had beautiful legs, lean and lightly muscled, legs that begged to be touched. He gave in to their allure, stroking the silken skin of her thigh, inching his hand ever upward. Slowly, carefully, he slipped beneath the thin cotton nightgown, his palm caressing the curve of her hip.

She felt like heaven.

He closed his eyes, overwhelmed by the need to make this woman his. He wanted her. He wanted her as desperately now as he had last night. She was his wife, dammit all. He could take her and no one would object—including his lovely bride. But to fondle her as she slept, when she wasn't in a position to object... What sort of lowlife was he? Using every ounce of strength, he removed his hand and opened his eyes.

Wynne's sleepy gaze met his.

Her expression held open curiosity, and he stilled, reining in his desires, forcing his features into an impassive mask. His control was pointless. She inhaled sharply, comprehension dawning with the first glimmer of morning light. Her spring-green eyes never wavered, hope shimmering in their depths, and she shifted closer, trapped within the stream of scarlet rays just peeking over the windowsill. Sunrise bathed her in a russet glow, licking across her hair and skin like a flame.

She greeted him with a shy smile. "Good morning, Mr. Hondo."

"Mornin', Mrs. Hondo," he replied gruffly. "How did you sleep?"

"Not bad. Thank you for joining me. I was afraid you wouldn't."

"I almost didn't."

"What changed your mind?"

"You asked so nicely. How could I refuse?"

She grinned in response and brushed a lock of hair from her eyes. The unstudied movement caused the bodice of her nightgown to gape, exposing her breasts. They were lovely, pale and round, the nipples the color of sun-ripened peaches. Unable to resist, he reached out and filled his palm, anticipating some sort of protest. It never came. Her only reaction was a muffled gasp, and then her eyes grew dark and slumberous.

He glanced down at his hand, his copper-tinged skin a sharp contrast to the pure whiteness of her breast. She was beautiful, beautiful to the eyes and exquisite to the touch. And as one timeless moment followed another, he silently raged at himself for allowing lust to overrule common sense. With a bitten off curse, he released her.

"Don't stop," she murmured shyly.

His mouth tightened. "You're joking, right?"

"I'm not afraid anymore."

He jackknifed upright, looming over her, infusing his voice with a strong warning. "You will be if I don't stop. I guarantee it."

"You wouldn't hurt me."

"Oh, no?" He laughed at her naivete, the sound barren and humorless. "We've had this conversation before, remember? I'm not capable of doing anything else."

"Others may believe that, but I don't." She reached
out, stroking the tense muscles of his arm. When he
didn't protest, she leaned closer, emboldened, pressing
feather-light kisses the length of his raspy jawline.

He managed to shove a single word past tightly
clenched teeth. "Don't."

"I just wanted to show I wasn't afraid."

"Aren't you?" It would be so easy to prove her wrong.
His resolve hardened. Maybe if he did, it would settle
the situation between them once and for all. He didn't
delay any further. In one lightning-fast move, he tossed
her backward. Crouching above, he planted his hands
on either side of her head, settling the lower half of his
body on top of hers. Only her cotton nightgown separated them. It was a flimsy barrier—about as flimsy as
his self-control. "Afraid now?" he demanded.

She shook her head, but he noticed that some of her
confidence had fled.

"You should be."

Shadows briefly marred the serenity of her expression
before vanishing in the face of absolute certainty. "I need
you, Jake." She reached for him, tracing the taut angles
of his face from cheekbone to chin. "And you need me."

The wild animal was back, feral gold eyes glaring down
at her. "Why are you doing this?" he snarled. "Don't
you understand? Don't you get it? This marriage should
never have happened. I'm not a safe man to be around."

"Do you want to hurt me?" she asked curiously.
"Does it give you pleasure to hurt people?"

A muscle jerked in his cheek. "No."

"Then don't."

"It's not that simple."

"Isn't it?" Her other hand settled on his hip, gliding
upward, tracing the contoured muscles from abdomen
to chest.

His breathing grew strained and he caught her hand, stilling its insidious exploration. "I can't... I don't... Damn, but you're pushing your luck."

"I guess I am. But tell me something.... If I said you were hurting me, would you stop?"

His throat worked for a moment as though answering were a struggle. Finally he nodded. "Yeah. I'd stop."

She smiled, her expression so radiant, it blinded him to everything else. "Then I'll make a deal with you. The minute you do something that hurts me, I'll ask you to stop. And if I do anything that hurts you, just say the word. All right?"

A harsh, disbelieving laugh burst from him. "You can't be serious—"

"I'm very serious." She gazed up at him, her eyes clear and direct. It was a probing look, one that threatened to pierce straight to his very soul—assuming he still had anything worthy of such a name. And then she said something that knocked him over the edge. "I trust you, Jake."

So simple. So absolute. So innocent and trusting. And so devastating. It broke him, splintering the rock-solid shell he'd spent his entire life erecting.

From the minute he'd seen her, he'd wanted her. Of course, it had been sheer desire, a physical need, savage and elemental and basic. He hadn't tried to fool himself about that—had never held with the sort of man who wrapped lust in pretty lies. No, he'd always been blunt and honest, both with himself and with his women. He took what he wanted without concern for the consequences before walking away—heart-whole and fancy-free. It had been his credo as long as he could remember.

But with Wynne...

He couldn't. He couldn't take her with the same thoughtless disregard. She wasn't like the other women he'd had. They'd all known the score. And if they'd secretly hoped to change his mind, he'd been quick to disabuse them of the notion.

"Jake?"

He fought for strength, fought harder than he ever had before. If he never committed another noble or honorable act again in his life, so help him, he'd get this one moment right. "Are you sure?"

"Positive."

"If you want me to stop, say the word and I'll stop." He hoped. With infinite care, he gathered her close. "Just do me one favor."

"What?"

"Don't wait too long. My off switch isn't all that trustworthy."

Her soft laugh was as arousing as a caress. "You won't need it. I promise."

"I hope you take your promises seriously," he muttered and lowered his head, kissing her with unchecked passion.

He was done talking. If he frightened her, it would be best to know now while he still had the self-possession to leave her untouched. But instead of pulling back, she wrapped her arms around him and gave him kiss for kiss.

Wynne was lost. Lost in a sensuous haze of mouths and tongues and tender caresses. She was still on her back, the hem of her nightgown drifting ever upward, the neckline falling further open. And always his hands— skating, probing, coasting over bared skin.

"Too many clothes," he muttered, the warmth of his breath catching in the hollow of her shoulder.

And then there weren't any clothes.

"Jake..." His name came out half-strangled. "Please."

"I want to please you. Tell me it's what you want, too." He surged upward, lifting half-off her. Cool air swirled into the breach, a biting foil to the explosive heat simmering between them. "What's your final answer, wife?"

"Wait..." She groaned in dismay, knowing that wasn't what she'd meant, that she'd only said it to keep him from leaving her side. Everything was so mixed up. So confused. Words didn't make sense any more. Nothing made sense...except for Jake.

"You want me to stop?" His voice sounded strained, urgent. "Don't play games with me, dammit!"

Her head shifted restlessly against the sheets. "No. Don't stop." Finally the words came out right, fervent in their demand. With an aggression that amazed her, she pulled him back into her arms, shifting to accommodate his weight. "Don't ever stop."

His mouth found hers, absorbing her whimpered pleas before slipping downward. He anointed her rounded contours with his tongue, savoring each gentle dip and curve as though it were an exotic spice. His touch left behind a trail of insidious devastation as he explored places never seen by a man, let alone kissed. And all the while a burning need licked at her. She trembled helplessly as Jake fed that fire, building it higher and brighter and hotter. Desire became a ravenous hunger unlike any she'd ever known, a hunger she'd do anything to sate.

"Jake!" She sobbed out his name, begging for that ultimate gratification.

"It's coming, sweetheart. I promise, it's coming."

Still his hands played, tripping along nerves stretched to the brink. As though sensing she'd reached the end of her endurance, he positioned himself between her thighs. For an endless moment she lay spread beneath him, trembling helplessly on the verge of some great cataclysm. Then he drove into her with one surging thrust.

He tensed as he absorbed the shock of her innocence, his eyes blazing like golden flames through a tumble of black hair. "What—"

"It's all right," she tried to reassure. "Please, Jake!"

Didn't he understand? The pain of his taking was nothing in comparison to the urgent need his possession had sparked. She smoldered with it. Desperate to convince him, she rocked her hips upward in silent appeal, begging for the completion hovering just out of reach. He wanted to pull away, she could tell, and she watched helplessly as he fought an inner battle, struggling to subdue the most powerful of nature's urges.

It was a battle he had no hope of winning.

"I can't," he muttered. "Heaven help me, I can't . . ."

He shut his eyes, fighting for restraint, fighting to make her passage as painless as possible. But restraint was also beyond him. The breath exploded from his chest and he drove into her heat. "Forgive me, elf," he gasped out the words. "I never meant for this to happen."

They rode the crest together, out of control and not caring. It was a magical experience, a melding of heart and body and soul. And just as the sun loosened its full glory on the pair of lovers, they found sweet deliverance within its circle of golden light.

Wynne didn't know how much time passed or how long they lay entwined in each others arms. But with the sating of their passion, sanity returned. Jake was the first to recover.

"You were a virgin," he accused, rolling free of her embrace.

Suddenly self-conscious, she tugged the sheet around her. Not that he seemed terribly concerned about modesty. "I didn't think you'd notice."

"You didn't think I'd . . ." Outrage battled disbelief. "Take my word for it, I noticed!"

"Does it matter that much?"

He came off the bed, snagging his robe from the floor as he did so. "We discussed this last night at the Montagues'," he said, thrusting his arm into the terry-cloth sleeve. "I told you flat out that I didn't want to be married to a virgin."

"Well... you're not. At least, not anymore."

His scalding invectives brought a rosy glow to her cheeks. "Don't split hairs with me, lady. Dammit all, I don't want to be saddled with a virgin. I wouldn't know what to do with one."

She gave him a mischievous grin. "What you just did suits me fine. And as I keep pointing out... It's no longer an issue."

"That's not what I meant!" His anger simmered visibly, like heat roiling in the desert air. "You lied to me. You said you'd been engaged three different times."

"I didn't lie. I *was* engaged three times."

"And not one of them... They never...?"

"Not one of them," she confirmed. "Ever."

"It staggers the imagination," he muttered, then grimaced. "That doesn't change the fact that I need an experienced woman. I need someone who's willing to admit in open court that I... That we..."

She tilted her head to one side. "Yes? That we... what?"

"That we—"

A loud banging sounded at the door. "Aunt Wynne! Aunt Wynne! Wake up."

Jake stiffened. "Now who the hell is that?" Laser-sharp eyes focused on her. "Something I should know about?"

Wynne swallowed nervously. She really wished she'd had a little more time to prepare him. Because she suspected that his annoyance over her innocence would be nothing compared to his annoyance over this next bit of news. Gathering every ounce of self-possession, she offered a tentative smile.

"*That*," she announced, "is my inheritance."

CHAPTER FOUR

NOT WAITING TO SEE how Jake would react to the news, Wynne jumped out of bed, dragging the sheet with her. Unlatching the door, she opened it a scant inch. "Hey, brat," she teased the boy planted squarely in front of the threshold. "You're up early."

"It weren't me," scorned Buster, hauling a younger boy out from behind him. "It was Chick. He got scared when he woke up and couldn't find you."

"What about Laura?" Wynne asked in concern. "She was there, wasn't she?"

Buster shrugged. "He didn't want Laura."

She switched her attention to the smaller of the two, and offered a reassuring smile, not at all surprised to see Chick's thumb firmly planted in his mouth. "Well, I'm here now. Just give me a minute to dress and I'll let you in so you can meet your new uncle, okay?"

That sparked some interest. "An uncle?" Buster questioned cautiously, exchanging a quick look with his brother. "How'd we get an uncle?"

"I married him last night. Remember? I told you I might. Now don't move. I'll be right back."

She decided not to introduce the boys to Jake until she'd changed into something more appropriate to a first meeting than a sheet. Leaving the door slightly ajar, she snatched up her overnight bag before shooting Jake a brief, nervous glance. He stood by the window facing her, his arms folded across his chest. His expression did not bode well for her future health.

Fleeing into the bathroom, she slammed the door closed. This was not good. She leaned against the cool, painted surface and nibbled her lower lip. How much had he heard and just how mad was he? Enough, she decided, and plenty mad. If she read that glitter in his eyes correctly, he was seriously ticked off. She sighed.

This was not going at all as she'd planned—except for last night and this morning. That had exceeded every dream she'd ever envisioned and then some. She shoved her wedding band more securely onto her finger, her movement reflected in the mirror over the sink. Curious, she dropped her bag and crept closer, studying herself for any changes the past few hours had wrought.

Her hair couldn't have been more rumpled if she'd just come in from a fast ride in an open convertible. Beneath wispy bangs, her eyes glowed a vivid green, brimming with happiness and startling in their intensity. She looked as though she'd found the key to all the secrets in the universe and then some. Well, maybe she had. She'd certainly found a whole new world locked within Jake's arms.

She adjusted her grip on the sheet and it dipped lower, exposing a small patch of reddened skin. It was a brand of possession—Jake's possession—and she swallowed, remembering the delicious rasp of his stubbled cheek against her breast.

Three different fiancés had attempted every wile under the sun to lure her into their beds and not once had she been tempted. But with Jake... No wiles. No lures. Just a passionate, irresistible man with wicked gold eyes and a touch that drove every thought but one from her head. And look where that one thought had led her—straight into marriage and then into his bed.

Had it been a mistake? She shook her head without a moment's hesitation. No. She hadn't made a mistake. She'd chosen a warrior to fight Mrs. Marsh and a husband who'd made her passage into marriage a memory more precious than anything that had gone before.

Jake pounded on the door. "Move it, elf," came his muffled order. "You can't hide in there forever. Get your tail out here and face the music."

She sighed. So much for precious memories.

Catapulted into action, she took the fastest shower on record and scrambled into her clothes, happiness gripping her despite her worries. The past twenty-four hours had been the most wondrous, enchanted moments of her entire life. And the idea of a future filled with equally wondrous, enchanted moments brought a silly grin to her mouth.

It disappeared the instant she stepped from the bathroom.

"Who the hell is the kid at the door?" Jake demanded.

She hesitated, casting him a quick, sidelong glance, noticing he'd also taken time to dress. Well-worn jeans clung to his lean hips, delineating the powerful length of his thighs. More distracting was his unbuttoned shirt, which did nothing to conceal the impressive breadth of his darkly furred chest.

"He's my nephew."

Jake's eyes narrowed as he shoved his feet into boots. "He has something to do with your inheritance?"

She shot a quick look at the gaping door, certain the boys were eavesdropping on every word of their conversation. "He *is* my inheritance, but, ah..." She wavered, torn between the desire to answer Jake's questions and her anxiety over leaving the boys standing in the hallway unattended. She'd learned from past experience that they didn't do well on their own. In fact, it was amazing they hadn't already lost patience with the delay and erupted into the room. "Could we discuss this later?"

"No. We'll discuss this right now."

"Then, could we make it fast? The boys are waiting."

"Tough," he retorted, then froze. "Whoa. Time out. You said boys. As in...plural? There's more than one of 'em?"

"There's two. Buster and Chick." She edged toward the door. "Look... They're my sister's kids. She and her husband were killed a year ago and I'm their guardian. At least they were left to me in Tracy's will. Unfortunately Mrs. Marsh—that's their other aunt—is doing everything in her power to gain custody of them. So, I married you to prevent her from succeeding. Okay?"

She never learned if he thought it was okay or not. Another knock sounded at the door and Wynne flung it wide before Jake could gather breath to protest. To her relief, Laura had joined the boys.

"About time," she groused, stepping into the room, a decidedly grumpy expression marring an otherwise pretty face. "The minute I turned my back, these two took off. Though how they found your room is beyond me."

"We asked the front desk," Buster explained. "They wouldn't tell us till I pinched Chick and he started hollerin'."

Chick sniffled in response, rubbing an apparently sore arm.

Jake took a step in their direction. "Would someone tell me what the hell—" Four sets of outraged eyes nailed him on the spot and he made a quick adjustment to his vocabulary. "What the...the *heck-fire* is going on?"

Laura gave Jake one long, horrified look before spinning to confront Wynne. "Please. Tell me this isn't your husband. He's not, is he?"

"Of course he's my husband." Wynne frowned. "Why?"

"Oh, no. This will never do."

"Finally," Jake said in satisfaction, folding his arms across his chest. "Someone who agrees with me."

"Why won't he do?" Wynne questioned. She stared at the man she'd married, searching for any visible flaws she might have overlooked the night before. As far as she could tell, there were none. He was as perfect now as he'd been when she'd first laid eyes on him.

"He's a Texan!" Laura stated as though that were explanation enough. "I'd know that accent anywhere."

"Now wait just a damn—darn minute," Jake growled, clearly insulted. "What's wrong with Texans?"

"Good question. What *is* wrong with Texans?" Wynne asked.

"What's wrong with them?" Laura grasped her friend's arm and hustled her to one side of the room. "Have you lost your mind?" she questioned in a distressed voice. "You can't throw a rope around a Texan and expect to lasso anything other than trouble."

"Don't be ridiculous," Wynne said with a laugh. "Jake won't give me a minute's trouble. He's here to help."

Jake stared at her in disbelief before informing her grimly, "Trust me, *wife*. The minute we're alone I intend to give you a sh—truckload of trouble. You lied to me. And I don't take kindly to lies."

"I didn't lie," she protested.

"Then you did some mighty fancy two-steppin' around the truth. In my book that's as good as a lie."

She sighed. "I just omitted one tiny detail."

"That detail being that your inheritance comes with arms, legs and a whole lot of aggravation in between. Why didn't you 'fess up last night?" He nailed her with a hard glare. "I'll tell you why. Because if you had, you knew I'd walk away. Hell, I'd probably have run."

Laura groaned. "You are in way over your head here," she warned.

"Everything will work out," Wynne insisted, glancing pointedly at the boys. She offered a bracing smile in the hopes of easing their worried expressions. "Jake and I just need to talk this through—alone and in private."

Laura gave a little snort. "A fat lot of good that'll do. You don't talk things over with Texans. They bark and you start jumping or suffer the consequences. I should know. I'm sorry to say I was married to one." She fixed Jake with a sour look. "Fortunately for my mental health it was brief. Very brief."

"Ah, jeez," Jake muttered in disgust.

"Just look at him," Laura continued as though he hadn't opened his mouth. "In case you failed to notice, this is one tough hombre. He's more outlaw than savior. Why, I'll bet the man eats nails for breakfast, shoe leather for dinner and bullets for between meal snacks."

"He hasn't eaten a single bullet that I'm aware of," Wynne retorted mildly. "Unless they were buried in the chocolate cake we had last night."

"They weren't," Jake reassured.

"You know what I mean," Laura snapped, glaring at him before returning her attention to Wynne. "He'll make mincemeat out of you in no time. And what about the boys?"

Wynne wrapped her arms around their shoulders, hugging them close. "What about them?"

"What sort of influence will he be on Chick and Buster?"

"A bad one," Jake admitted.

"Terrible," Laura concurred. "I suggest an immediate annulment. We'll find some other way to take care of Mrs. Marsh."

"Forget it."

"Not a chance."

Wynne smiled at her husband, pleased that they were in temporary accord. "There, you see?" she said. "He's a man of his word. He promised to help me keep my inheritance and that's what he'll do. He's just a little surprised at what it entailed."

"That's the understatement of the century," Jake said.

"And how do you know that the minute Mrs. Marsh shows up, he won't dump you like all the others?" Laura questioned sharply.

"Because we made a deal." Wynne's voice reflected her absolute faith. "He has too much honor and integrity to leave me and the boys at the mercy of Mrs. Marsh. Right, Jake?"

He shut his eyes and rubbed a spot between his brows with his thumb. "I knew I should have kept walkin' the instant I saw her heading my way," he muttered. "Why didn't I?"

Wynne smiled. "Because I needed you and you needed me."

"No." Eyes as bright and golden as the midday sun seared her with unrelenting heat. "It's because I let the wrong part of my anatomy do my thinking for me."

"Wynne... Get out of this marriage before it's too late," Laura pleaded.

"I can't." Her gaze never left Jake's. "If I leave him, he'll lose his inheritance."

"So what? Let him. He's strong. He's tough. He can take care of himself."

"I'm sure he can," Wynne admitted with a wry smile.

"Then why go through with this?" Laura pressed. "Because you're wrong, you know. He doesn't need you. His sort doesn't need anyone."

"That's where you're wrong. He may not know it, but I have something he lacks, something he wants."

Laura groaned in frustration. "Open your eyes. Look at all you stand to lose if you go through with this. If you won't do what's best for yourself, then at least think about what's best for the boys."

Wynne spared her friend a brief glance. "I am thinking of the boys," she said gently. "In fact they're my sole consideration. They need a man in their life, a role model, someone they can look up to and emulate. Someone who can protect them." Her gaze swung back to Jake. "And that's exactly what I've gotten."

He flinched as though she'd struck him. "You don't know what you're talking about."

"Don't I?" She came to a decision. "Laura, please take the children back to our room," she instructed. "Jake and I need to discuss this privately. I'll join you there as soon as I can."

Laura planted her hands on her hips. "And leave you alone with this...this *Texan*?" She shook her head. "Not a chance."

"There's nothing he can do to me that hasn't already been done."

"Don't count on it," Jake inserted.

"What about us?" Buster asked, dropping into the conversation. "Is that man gonna be our uncle or what? Chick wants to know."

"And I'll have an answer for Chick in a little while," Wynne replied. "But first I need to talk to Jake."

Laura took a deep breath and slowly released it. "All right, Wynne. We'll do it your way. The boys and I will go back to the room...on one condition."

"Which is?"

"I want you to take a good, long look at Mr. Texan over there. You told me you were going to marry a Prince Charming." She stabbed a finger in Jake's direction. "Well, that's not him. And if you give him half a chance, I'm sure he'll prove it to you." With that she grasped each boy by the hand and hustled them through the door, slamming it behind her.

A tense silence descended, and Wynne took the opportunity to do as Laura had requested. She studied Jake curiously, wondering what qualities her friend had seen that had escaped her own discerning gaze.

True, at first glance he was an intimidating man. His height and breadth alone might give some people pause, especially when combined with his strange golden eyes—eyes that could change from arctic cold to broiling heat in the space of an instant. And she supposed that his shadowed jaw and rumpled hair gave him the appearance of a man more comfortable living outside the boundaries of convention. But where Laura saw a hard, ruthless Texan, Wynne saw a strong, determined protector.

In fact the only difference she noticed since last night was the distrustful expression that now glittered in his eyes—a deep-seated wariness mixed with jaded cynicism. She recognized that look. Jake had had close and personal experience with bitter disappointment and expected to again in the near future.

From her? she couldn't help but wonder.

He stood off to one side of the room, his jaw set at a combative angle, his body tensed in anticipation of a blow. It struck her as a customary stance for him, one he'd probably assumed with distressing frequency. He was demon-ridden, she sensed, battling both outer and inner conflicts. And it saddened her. Had he always been a loner, at odds with the world, forced to fight his way through life? Somehow she suspected he had.

"Why would you be a bad influence on the boys?" she asked abruptly.

"What?"

She crossed to the bed and perched on the end of it. "Laura said you'd be a bad influence on Buster and Chick and you agreed with her. Why?"

"Because I don't know anything about kids or how to raise them."

"You were once a boy. Why can't you—"

"Take a page from what passed as my childhood?" Darkness descended on him. "You wouldn't want that. Not when it comes to my fathering someone you cared about."

She regarded him curiously. "Would you hurt the boys?"

"Not on purpose."

"Then—"

"That's not the point." He ran a hand through his hair, impatience edging his voice. "I attended that asinine party because I needed a temporary wife in order to gain control of my inheritance. To be brutally frank, I didn't give a damn who I married so long as she'd stick with me until the terms of the will were fulfilled."

"No problem."

"Big problem," he corrected. "You need a real husband. A full-time, forever type to give those kids a stable home. Well, I'm not it."

"You could be."

He shook his head in disgust. "Boy, are you barking up the wrong tree," he muttered. Taking a deep breath, he fixed her with a stern, no-nonsense stare. "This isn't some sort of fairy tale wedding, you know. There aren't any happy endings waiting around the next bend in the road. If you'd been straight with me from the beginning, told me what your inheritance was, you'd have saved us both a lot of trouble."

"This may not be what you initially anticipated, but—"

"It's nothing like I anticipated," he cut in. "I require a wife in my house—and my bed—for a brief stint. Period. End of relationship."

"And I've agreed to that," she insisted doggedly.

"Have you?" He ate up the distance separating them in two swift strides. Clasping her shoulders, he hauled her to her feet, looking every inch the menacing outlaw Laura had accused him of being. "I want a woman in my life for as long as necessary and then I want her gone. No complications. No regrets. And no future. When our time is through, I'm walking away and I won't be looking back."

She nodded, her wide gaze glued to his. "You told me that already."

His mouth thinned. "But you weren't listening, were you? You've had your head in the clouds for so long, you couldn't find the ground if you landed on it face-first. And now I'm saddled with a wife who believes in fairy tales and a couple of kids in desperate need of a father."

"That's what I'd have preferred," she admitted, "but I'm willing to—"

"To what?" he demanded. "Continue playing your little games after I take you home with me? What's the plan now... to try to get me to agree to something more permanent over the next few months?"

She didn't dare admit the truth. Instead she gave a forlorn little shrug. "It doesn't matter what I'd hoped, Jake. I realize now it was a foolish dream. We'll do it your way."

"You're damned right we will. But just to set the record straight... let's hear the truth." He grasped her chin and forced her to meet his eyes. "You deliberately kept silent about those kids. And you did it because you knew it would be too risky to explain their existence before that wedding band hit your finger. Have I missed anything?"

Guilt swamped her. Her expression must have given her away because his eyes iced over. Why, oh why had she agreed to Laura's stipulation? she wondered miserably. Judging by the look on Jake's face, it had been a costly error. She took a deep breath. "Yes, I deliberately didn't tell you about Buster and Chick. But I would have been up-front about it. At least, I would have if I hadn't already lost three fiancés as a result of that sort of honesty."

His hands tightened, anger rippling across his countenance. "You didn't tell me about those kids, because you accurately guessed that I'd never have married you. Then you wore that damned nightgown in an attempt to seduce me, knowing full well I'd do anything to have you. And once I'd had you, I'd be stuck with our bargain. Isn't that right, my sweet little virgin?"

She shook her head frantically, appalled by his reasoning. "No. That's not true. You said you needed to consummate the marriage. I was just—"

"Sacrificing yourself for the sake of the boys?" His mouth curled to one side. "How noble."

Tears gathered in her eyes, but she stubbornly refused to let them fall. "I've done everything you've requested. You warned me our marriage would only be temporary and I've agreed. You asked that we consummate the marriage and I did. What more do you want from me?"

His gaze turned steamy. "It isn't complicated. You figure it out," he retorted.

"I mean...does our marriage stand or not?" she asked bluntly.

With a muttered exclamation, he released her. "I don't have much choice. If I let you go, I lose everything. And I'm too close to winning to allow that to happen." He crossed to the window and stared out at the landscape for endless moments before swinging around to face her. "Okay. The marriage stands. But fair warning. You deceived me once. Don't let it happen again. You won't like the consequences."

His threat barely impinged as she struggled to conceal her jubilation. "Fine," she agreed. "And just so you know... I would have been frank about the boys if you'd asked." She lifted her chin. "But you didn't."

His eyes narrowed, reflecting his skepticism. "I guess we'll never know for sure, will we?" He didn't give her a chance to debate the issue. "Well, wife, what now? I can't say this is a very auspicious beginning to our relationship."

Reluctantly Wynne allowed him to change the subject. Besides, what good would debating the point do? He'd never believe her. "All I have asked—and still do ask— is that you protect us from Mrs. Marsh."

He released a gusty sigh. "I'm supposed to slay your dragons, is that it?"

Wynne nodded. "That's it."

"Tell me about this Mrs. Marsh. Who is she?"

"She's the boys' aunt, my brother-in-law's sister."

"And you call her *Mrs*. Marsh?"

"She discourages familiarity," Wynne explained wryly. "And she has both the money and the power to indulge her preferences. Right now the preference she's indulging is a powerful maternal streak, and she's not happy that Tracy and Rob appointed me the boys' guardian."

"How did they die?"

"In a car crash." Her expression turned somber. "Chick was with them when it happened. He hasn't spoken since—except to Buster."

"Poor kid." Sympathy intensified the grim lines bracketing his mouth. "What's with the odd names? Or are they nicknames?"

"Nicknames. Benjamin Curtis and Charles William, alias Buster and Chick. Buster is eight and Chick just turned five. They're very close."

"I noticed. They never strayed more than a foot apart." He hooked a thumb through his belt loop and eyed her intently. "You ever have them in for counseling?"

She nodded. "Buster seems to have made quite a bit of progress, but Chick... Aside from the trauma of the accident, I think he's also afraid Mrs. Marsh will get hold of them again."

"Again?"

"She took care of them for several weeks right after the accident."

"Is she really that bad?"

Wynne shrugged. "She means well, I suppose... But we have our differences. One problem is that I've been home-schooling them this year because they couldn't bear to be separated. Mrs. Marsh objected. She feels the boys would be better off in a private school. It's one her brother attended, but neither of them wants to go. Nor do I think it would be a smart choice right now. Plus, she's... well, she's rather strict."

"Strict isn't bad."

Wynne sighed. "You'd have to meet her to understand."

"I gather she wants custody?"

"Yes. After her brother died, she threatened to take me to court in order to keep the children. I've spent the last year doing everything I could to prevent that from happening."

"Not an easy task."

"No." That one word spoke volumes. "Besides the issue of school, finances are tight. Rob and Tracy left some insurance money in trust for the boys." Wynne made a face. "Mrs. Marsh had it frozen. Even if she hadn't, I wouldn't have wanted to dip into the money. Better it be saved for their education."

"But it's made supporting them difficult," he guessed.

"I've managed."

"You're working like a dog and are broke. Is that about the size of it?"

He saw far too much, she realized uneasily. "Yes," she admitted. "I'm afraid it is."

"So your solution is to marry?"

She shot him a direct look. "I wasn't after a meal ticket, if that's what you're suggesting. The reason for the marriage was Mrs. Marsh. If I have a husband, she no longer has grounds for going after the children."

"And without one?"

"She has a case," Wynne admitted grudgingly.

He took a minute to absorb the information, then nodded. "Okay. If this marriage is going to work—even temporarily—we'll both have to do our part. So... For the length of our association I'll do my best to protect you and the boys from Mrs. Marsh."

"And I'll uphold my end of the bargain, as well."

He cupped her face between callused hands. "This isn't what I'd planned. You know that, don't you?"

She could hear the frustration underlining his quietly spoken question, the thread of anger he still hadn't mastered. And yet his eyes revealed another emotion altogether, one of blatant desire—a potent, overwhelming need he seemed helpless to control. Her reaction followed swiftly. Warmth pooled in the pit of her stomach, spreading outward with each beat of her heart. A helpless lassitude paralyzed her limbs, holding her in place. Even if she'd wanted to, she couldn't have pulled free of his grasp.

"Jake..." she whispered.

His laugh was half groan. "I know, elf. I know. I don't understand it, either."

He nuzzled the curve of her throat, just below her ear and she gasped, her eyes falling closed. He hadn't buttoned his shirt and she spread her hands across his chest, fanning her fingers through the generous mat of hair. Her palms tingled from the delicious abrasion as she followed the compact line of muscles from shoulder to abdomen. He felt wonderful, strong and hard and deliciously male.

"You drive me crazy," he muttered.

Thrusting his hands beneath the bottom of her blouse, he skimmed the length of her spine until he found the fastening for her bra. With one quick flick, he unhooked it, freeing her breasts for a more thorough exploration. It was still too restrictive, the fitted blouse too great a barrier. He didn't waste time unfastening the buttons, but simply yanked her top over her head, baring her to his heated gaze.

"Jake—"

Dark color emphasized the high arch of his cheekbones. "Don't fight me. Not now."

"We can't." The objection sounded reluctant even to her own ears. "Laura and the boys are waiting."

"Let 'em wait."

"They might come back."

"I'll lock the door." He cupped her softness, his eyes a molten gold. "They'll get the message when we don't answer."

She struggled to think, to put words into a coherent whole. "You don't know Laura," she managed to say. "She's tenacious."

"We'll hang up the Do Not Disturb sign. She's no fool. She'll understand."

"That's what I'm worried about."

"Forget Laura," he demanded, passion adding a husky edge to his voice. "I have something more interesting in mind."

With that, his mouth closed over hers and all thought ended. Desire blossomed with stunning speed, returning more swiftly than before, burning higher and with greater ferocity. How was it possible to feel so at one with a man she'd only known for a few short hours?

"I've never seen a more perfectly made woman." His heated breath mingled with hers. "If it weren't for those kids, our time together would be downright perfect."

With those few heartfelt words he destroyed all her illusions, proving beyond a doubt how wrong she'd been about their relationship. Having a bucket of ice-cold water tipped over her head couldn't have sliced through her sensuous haze any more thoroughly. The air escaped her lungs in a harsh gasp. "Say you don't mean that," she whispered, distressed beyond measure.

It took him a minute to hear the misery in her voice, to realize she was no longer an active participant in their lovemaking. His muscles tensed as he fought to control his desire. Taking a deep breath, he pulled back, a rush of cool air filling the chasm between them.

"What?"

"Your comment about the children... Say you didn't mean it."

"You want me to lie?" he questioned sharply. "You want me to say that I'm thrilled to be saddled with a wife and two kids I'd never planned on having? Sorry. I'm not putting a pretty face on an ugly truth. I want you. No question about that. But I'd have been a whole hell of a lot happier if there weren't any strings attached."

She jerked free of his hold and swept up her blouse. "Everything comes at a price," she informed him tautly, dressing with more speed than grace.

"I'm well aware of that." A wealth of meaning lay buried in his retort, a history she could only guess at. "But you didn't tell me the cost until it was too late for a refund."

"Or you'd never have made the purchase?" she asked, bracing herself, as though in anticipation of a blow.

He didn't answer. Crossing the room, he picked up a canvas tote and his Stetson. "You ready to leave? Looks like we're done here."

She didn't bother arguing. Grabbing her overnight bag and purse, she nodded. "I'm ready," she said, following him to the door. "Though you haven't told me where we're going yet."

He paused. "Texas, as your friend so accurately guessed. Chesterfield, Texas, to be precise. I own a spread there."

She stared in wonder. "A ranch." It was almost too good to be true. "What a wonderful place to raise children."

His face darkened, his eyes deepening to a tarnished bronze. "I'll have to take your word for it. I was raised in the city." He yanked the door open, then hesitated, tossing the words over his shoulder. "Fair warning, wife. I'll do whatever's necessary to make this marriage as comfortable for you as possible. But don't expect me to give you what I don't have."

"You mean love?" she dared to ask.

"Love's an illusion," he retorted coldly. Then his voice dropped, turning gritty with tension. "Funny thing, illusions. No matter how hard you work at it, you can't believe them into existence. Try it and you'll end up with a world of hurt."

And with that, he walked out the door.

CHAPTER FIVE

THEY FLEW TO TEXAS on a large, commercial carrier, switching to a private puddle-jumper for the flight to Chesterfield. Jake had a pickup waiting for them at the tiny landing strip.

"Everybody in the front cab," he instructed, before glancing at Wynne. "It'll be a tight fit. But it's safer than putting the boys in the back with the luggage." He dumped their three small suitcases in the bed of the truck. "You didn't bring much with you."

She shrugged, her attention focused on Chick. He still had trouble riding in cars, and she wasn't certain how he'd take to the pickup. "I thought it would be easier to travel light. The rest of our belongings are packed and ready to be shipped once I supply the moving company with an address."

"You can phone them as soon as we get to the house," he said as he opened the passenger door. "Come on boys, shake a leg."

She held her breath, waiting to see what Chick would do. To her relief, he clambered inside without hesitation. Apparently the truck didn't rouse the same frightening memories as a car.

Jake turned to face her, lifting an eyebrow in question. "What's the matter?" he asked in an undertone.

She looked at him, startled. "You don't miss much, do you?"

His mouth curved into a wry smile. "Depends on how distracted I am. Is there something wrong with Chick?"

83

She shrugged. "Cars don't always agree with him," she explained quietly. "They...upset him."

Jake didn't appear surprised by her comment. "No problem. I don't own a car." He helped her into the cab. "And, since the pickup doesn't cause the same reaction, I'll let you drive it while you're here."

She poked her head out of the window. "But, what about you?"

"I have an old rust-bucket that I can use in the meantime. Or there's always my horse." With that he circled the truck and climbed behind the steering wheel. "Everybody ready? Seat belts fastened?"

"We're set, Uncle Jake," Buster said. "Where's your ranch? Chick wants to know."

"Not far. It'll take about a half hour to get there."

The time passed quickly, the boys watching every move Jake made with avid interest. Two minutes from the airport, the questions began—questions he answered simply and directly. Despite his annoyance over having acquired a ready-made family, he had been kindness itself to the boys on the flight—holding Chick's hand and listening to Buster's endless running commentary with amazing patience.

Clearly the boys had developed a severe case of hero worship—which worried her. Although Jake was eminently suited to such a role, he wouldn't be in their lives for long. She sighed. She'd taken great pains to explain that their new uncle was only a temporary addition to their family. But she wasn't convinced they'd believed her. And why should they, when she didn't believe it herself?

Twenty minutes later, they passed through a small town. "This is Chesterfield," Jake volunteered with notable reluctance.

Wynne looked around eagerly, deciding the town had an abundance of character. It was small, but attractive, all the shops freshly whitewashed and accented with either shutters or awnings or flower boxes. A clapboard livery with tall barnlike doors was sandwiched between an old-fashioned barber shop and a contemporary boutique. Across the street a general store with a two-story nineteenth-century facade stood cheek and jowl with a brand-new stucco bank. Most incongruous of all, a modern brick and glass structure housing a law firm sat opposite an outdoor market selling everything from flowers and produce to Mexican blankets and straw baskets.

It was unlike any place she'd ever seen. Horses were hitched in parking spaces alongside cars. A huge bronze statue commemorating the Texas Rangers had been planted in the middle of the road. And an honest-to-goodness saloon with real swinging doors graced one end of town. It even had a cowboy lounging outside in a rocker. Best of all the Lone Star flag snapped proudly above the small courthouse.

"This is Chesterfield?" she questioned in wonder. "It's beautiful."

"Avoid it," Jake retorted with a sharp edge. "There's a sizable town about forty minutes south of the ranch called Two Forks. It has everything you need—lots of malls and movie houses and such. You can go there whenever you get an itch to explore."

She twisted in her seat to catch a final glimpse of Chesterfield as it disappeared from view. "But why would I want to go to Two Forks when I could come here instead?"

"Because I said so."

And that apparently ended the discussion. She frowned. He'd have to get over these autocratic ways of his and soon. She'd been remarkably tolerant, knowing that by marrying her he'd taken on far more than he'd planned. Still... That didn't mean that she'd jump every time he barked a command, or obey without question or comment.

"Is that it?" Buster asked just then. He leaned forward, staring out the windshield. "Is that your ranch?"

"Yeah. That's it. Welcome to Lost Trail Ranch." Jake spared Wynne a quick, cryptic glance. "I know it needs some repairs—"

"I think it's wonderful," she exclaimed.

"Look, Chick. There's a barn and everything," Buster said, pointing. "You have horses, Uncle Jake? And cows and pigs?"

"No pigs. It's a ranch, not a farm. But there's plenty of cows and horses."

He turned down a long dirt driveway that divided an endless expanse of pastureland and parked outside the ranch house. The boys tumbled from the truck and scampered up the sagging porch steps while Jake unloaded the suitcases. Wynne followed behind, bemused by her good fortune.

She'd married a man with a house. How lucky could she get? They'd be living in a real two-story, multi-room residence instead of a cramped apartment. She fought to control the surge of tears stinging her eyes.

"It even has an upstairs!" Buster informed his brother. "Come on." He grabbed Chick's hand and disappeared into the cavernous interior.

Jake stepped across the threshold, then glanced her way. His set jaw and rigid stance spoke more loudly than words—he didn't like having her here. With a tiny sigh, she entered the house and looked around. The glaring afternoon sunlight followed them through the open doorway, cruelly accentuating the scarred pine floor and peeling wallpaper. Cobwebs trailed from the ceiling corners in ghostly tendrils and dust lay like a dingy gray blanket on every conceivable surface. Even the furniture was secondhand, mismatched and faded from use.

The house reminded her of a woman who, tired and careworn after years of hard living, had given up the effort.

"Look . . ." he said in an undertone. "I know it's run-down—"

"It's beautiful," she whispered, seeing only the possibilities. "It just needs some tender loving care to give it new life."

"It's a dump. I just moved back in and haven't had a chance—"

"Look at the size of the rooms. Compared to where we were living, it's a palace." She tilted her head. "And those ceilings . . . They're so high."

"I know you're upset," Jake began.

"Where's the kitchen?"

He pointed to the right. "But it's only for a short time."

"You've got plenty of food supplies," she said, checking the cupboards. "Rags?"

"Through that far door. In the mudroom." He stood in the middle of the kitchen, looking around in distaste. "I can hire some people to come out and help clean up a little."

"You even have a washer and dryer! I can't believe it." She practically danced across the kitchen floor. "And is that a fire-burning stove? I've never seen one before. How does it work?"

"Wood-burning," he said, correcting her. "It's a wood-burning stove and I'd rather you not fool with it. I'll get a microwave in here and you can cook with that."

"Oh, Jake. This is wonderful. A little soap and elbow grease and you won't recognize the place."

"I didn't marry you because I wanted a maid," he said more sharply than he'd intended.

Her smile didn't dim. "I know why you married me." She threw her arms around his neck. "A clean house will be my way of saying thank-you. I couldn't have asked for a more perfect home."

He muttered something beneath his breath and wrestled free of her stranglehold. Grasping her hands in his, he held her at a safe distance. "You don't need to put on an act for me. I know what this place looks like. It's a wonder you haven't turned tail and run." His mouth tightened. "But then, where would you go?"

She shrugged. "I haven't a clue. But fortunately that's not a problem." She gazed up at him with eyes as clear and vivid as spring grass, and a face as open and innocent as a newborn. "You couldn't have given me anything nicer than this."

Feeling like a total heel, he released her and stepped back. "I'm going out," he informed her gruffly.

"Okay. When will you return?"

"I don't know."

"Well . . . While you're gone I'll just run into town for supplies."

"No!" His hands balled into fists as he fought for control. "I mean, you can get supplies at the supermarket in Two Forks. When you get to the end of the driveway, turn left."

"Right."

"No, left. Got it? Left."

She grinned. "Gotcha."

He thrust a hand through his hair. "I'll hire some people to clean the house. And I'll pick up dinner at the local takeout. You don't need to worry about a thing."

It was the least he could do, considering his duplicity. A tight knot formed in the pit of his stomach. Why was he doing this? Why drop her in a house that should have been condemned years ago when he could put her up in a place worthy of a queen? He knew why. If he took her anywhere else, it would give her false hope. It would suggest a permanence he could never allow. Didn't she understand? He wasn't the marrying kind. Eventually he'd let her down. He'd shatter every hope and dream she'd ever possessed. And he couldn't bear to look into those huge, limpid eyes of hers when he destroyed that final illusion. No. Once she'd been mired in this hellhole for a while, she'd be desperate to leave.

And maybe one or two of those dreams would remain intact when she did.

"Why don't you look the place over and make a list of what you need?" His voice grated like steel wool on rust. "If you hit a snag, Dusty can help out. He should be around here someplace."

"Dusty?"

"My foreman. Big hat, little guy. Spits a lot. You can't miss him."

She grinned. "He sounds like quite a character."

"Yeah. He's a character, all right." Unable to help himself, he swept her into his arms and kissed her with unmistakable desperation. "You shouldn't have married me," he muttered when he finally released her. "You'll live to regret it. I guarantee."

"The only regrets I'll have is when it's time to leave."

He closed his eyes. "But you will leave," he told her in an inflexible voice.

"Do I have a choice?"

He hardened himself against the wistful plea tugging at the chip of stone that had once passed for his heart. "No. You don't," he said and walked out the door.

"Uh-oh," Wynne murmured as she gripped the steering wheel and stared at her feet.

"What's wrong?" Buster demanded.

Chick pointed at the pedals on the floor.

Buster frowned. "There's three." He eyed his aunt, a concerned expression creeping across his face. "You know how to drive a three-pedal car?"

She sighed. "'Fraid not."

"That's okay. I watched how Uncle Jake did it. And Dad's car had an extra petal, too." He stabbed a finger toward the first one. "That there makes it go. The middle makes it stop. And you push in that last one when you move this stick." He yanked on the gear shift to demonstrate.

"I had that much figured out." She gnawed on her lower lip. "Maybe we should wait until Jake gets back. I don't think I can make it all the way into Two Forks on my own."

"I don't wanna go to Two Forks, anyway," Buster retorted. "And neither does Chick. Let's go to that other town. The one with the cowboy statue. We like that town."

"Me, too," Wynne confessed.

"It's not far. You can do it."

Chick nodded enthusiastically.

"Okay," she said with as much optimism as she could scrape together. "Here goes."

She pushed in the clutch and turned the key, giving the engine some gas. It roared to life. But the second she lifted her foot off the clutch the car lurched to a stop and stalled.

"You gotta push hard on the gas and let that other one out real slow," Buster instructed.

Wynne shook her head. "I don't know. I'm not sure about this."

Chick patted her on the shoulder, his big blue eyes mirroring his absolute faith in her ability. With a sigh, she tried again and managed to keep the truck going long enough to turn it in a wide half circle. Engine screaming, they bounced down the dirt driveway.

"Move the stick!" shouted Buster.

Pushing in the clutch, she jerked the stick into a new setting. The pickup bucked angrily and stalled yet again, rolling to a halt at the end of the driveway.

"You're...ah...you're getting better," Buster lied unconvincingly.

"But not good enough to risk going all the way to Two Forks, right?" she said dryly.

"No way."

Chick shook his head emphatically.

"I guess that narrows our choices down to one. Chesterfield. Agreed?"

"Agreed," Buster confirmed.

Restarting the engine, she ground her way into first and turned to the right. Four stalls later, they reached the outskirts of town. The pickup jerked to a stop in front of the outdoor market and, deciding she'd pushed her luck as far as it would go, she coasted into a parking spot.

"Made it," Wynne said with undisguised relief. "But there's one small problem."

"What's that?" Buster demanded.

"I don't know how to do reverse. We may be stuck here a while." She brightened. "In the meantime, let's find that general store. We have shopping to take care of."

Jake turned his back on the window overlooking the colorful booths of the outdoor market and thrust his hands into his pockets. "It isn't going to work, Peter. This marriage is a total disaster."

Alarm appeared on the lawyer's face. "What happened? Wouldn't she sign the prenuptial agreement?"

"She signed it."

"She knows the marriage is temporary? Is she going to create a scene when it's time for a divorce?"

"She's agreed to the divorce, and she won't kick up a fuss."

"What about fulfilling the conditions of the will? You two are...ah...wedded and bedded, right?"

Jake gritted his teeth, pushing the words out with an effort. "It's been taken care of."

"And she'll admit as much? In open court?"

Jake's mouth tightened. "We haven't discussed it, yet. But knowing Wynne, she'll do anything I ask."

Peter stared, nonplussed. "Even a real wife wouldn't do that. Where's the problem? Your bride sounds damn near perfect to me."

"She's... Nice."

"Hell. That *is* a problem."

"I don't need your sarcasm, Bryant," Jake growled. "I'm serious. I'm in a real fix here."

"How? You wanted a plain, practical and levelheaded woman who'd agree to a temporary arrangement. Isn't that what you got?"

Jake frowned. "She isn't exactly plain," he admitted.

"No? You roped a pretty one, huh? What did you say her name was? Wynne?"

"Wynne Sommers. And she's..." Beautiful. Gorgeous. Sweet. *Innocent.*

"Practical?"

Jake couldn't help smiling. "Not that I've noticed." Determined. Whimsical. Adorable. *A starry-eyed dreamer.*

"But at least she's levelheaded."

When her head wasn't in the clouds—a rare occurrence he suspected. "She's hard to describe."

Peter didn't bother to hide his confusion. "Uh-huh. Give it a shot, anyway."

"She's..."

*　　*　　*

"Nuts. Wait a minute, boys. We have another problem." Wynne opened her purse and thumbed through her wallet, counting the last few dollars she had to her name. "Thirteen, fourteen, fifteen. Fifteen dollars and sixty-seven cents. That's not going to go very far."

"Can you write a check?" Buster asked, ever practical.

"I closed my Maryland bank account. But maybe…" She grasped the boys by the hand and marched toward the front of the store. "Excuse me," she said to the woman behind the cash register. "Is the owner here?"

"You're speakin' to her, honey. Belle Blue's the name. What can I do you for?"

"I'm Wynne Hondo. And these are my nephews, Buster and Chick. We just moved to Chesterfield and I came shopping while my husband ran errands and—"

"Did you say Hondo?" Belle repeated sharply.

"That's right." Wynne smiled in delight. "Do you know Jake?"

"Black hair, a heart of stone and the devil's own eyes? Sure, I know him."

Wynne frowned. "I think you must have him confused with someone else. Jake does have dark hair, but he's the kindest man in the world. And his eyes are the most beautiful shade of gold I've ever seen."

Belle stared in disbelief. "Somebody's confused, that's for darned sure. Who did you say you were?"

"Wynne Hondo."

"And you're Jake's…" She seemed to have trouble getting the appropriate word out.

"Wife. Yes. We just got married."

The woman eyed her suspiciously. "You have proof of that?"

"I think so." Wynne dug in her purse, searching for the envelope she'd been given by the county clerk.

"Asa, come over here and listen to this," the woman called out. "Jake's gone and got himself a wife." She shook her head in wonder as a tall, gray-haired man joined them. "And Randolph claimed there wouldn't be time enough. He is gonna be fit to be tied."

Locating the gold-leafed certificate, Wynne offered it to Belle, aware that a small, curious crowd had started to collect around the register. "This is just for decoration, you understand. It's not a legal document and I'm not supposed to pass it off as one, but—"

"Honey, any woman brave enough to throw a lasso around a man like Jake Hondo deserves a frame for that piece of paper—legal or otherwise. Consider it a wedding present from me and Asa."

"Why, thank you. That's very kind of you." Wynne's smile wavered. "But I still have a small problem."

"How can I help?"

"I only have fifteen dollars and sixty-seven cents on me and I wondered—"

"We'll put your purchases on Jake's tab. No problem." She winked. "It's not like we won't know where to find you when the bill comes due at the end of the month. That Chesterfield spread sure is a beauty, isn't it?"

Wynne stared at the woman in bewilderment. "Excuse me?"

"The Chesterfield spread. The ranch house where you're living."

"Oh, you must mean Lost Trail. The boys and I love it."

Belle gave her a strange look. "You're stayin' at Jake's old place?"

"Well, it does need a lick and a shine." A small murmur ran through the crowd of shoppers. "But we'll get it into shape in no time," she hastened to reassure.

"Oh, you will, will you?" Belle shook her head and muttered, "That Jake Hondo is some piece of work."

Wynne laughed. "He's something else, isn't he?"

*　　*　　*

"She's... She's something else," Jake finally said.

"And this—something else—is a problem," Peter guessed, still struggling to uncover the source of Jake's displeasure. "I don't understand. Didn't she like the Chesterfield spread?"

"I don't know. We're living at my place."

Peter stared, openmouthed. "You... you took her to that dump? Have you lost your mind? No wonder she's upset. Take her to Chesterfield Ranch. She'll cheer right up."

If he took her to his grandfather's house, she'd never leave—an untenable situation. Because one day soon the knight's armor in which she'd sheathed him would begin to show its tarnish. And he couldn't bear to live with her eventual disillusionment when she finally saw the man beneath the chain mail—the real man.

"Wynne's not upset," he retorted. "In fact, she likes my place. She's thrilled to be living in a house instead of an apartment. She's even going to clean it for me."

"*What*!"

"Not that I'd let her," he added defensively. "Which reminds me. I need to hire somebody to knock the place into shape. Give me some recommendations, will you?"

Peter wrinkled his brow in confusion. "Let me get this straight... You don't like this woman, right?"

"I didn't say that."

"But you're not in love with her."

Jake turned his back on Peter and poured himself a drink. It took a quick swig and several minutes of intense concentration to throw off a cool and adamant, "No."

"And she's thrilled to be living in that pigsty you call a house? She'll even clean it for you?"

Jake shrugged. "I gather her previous accommodations weren't as spacious." He thought of her labor-roughened hands. "Nor is she afraid of hard work."

"And she's not bad looking?"

Hair the color of moonlight, skin as pure and soft as virgin wool, eyes as serene as a forest glade. "She's beautiful," Jake admitted roughly.

"I want her."

"*What*!"

"After your divorce, I want her. She sounds like a dream come true."

"Go to hell, Bryant," Jake snapped, and turned to stare out the window.

Wynne shook hands for the umpteenth time, introducing herself and the boys to yet another resident of Chesterfield. "This has to be the friendliest town in the whole world," she marveled as she pushed her cart down the aisle.

"Kinda crowded," Buster observed, dodging another shopper.

"I guess they didn't feel like driving all the way into Two Forks any more than we did."

"How come everyone wants to shake hands with us? Nobody ever did that when we went shopping in Maryland."

"I guess that's the way people do things in Texas." She paused by the local bulletin board and studied the various announcements. "There's a charity craft fair next weekend. I wonder if Jake's donated anything. Maybe I can bake a cake if he hasn't."

Chick tugged on her arm and Buster said, "Chick wants you to bake cookies instead of cake. That way we can help fix 'em."

"Help eat them, you mean," she said with a laugh. "Well, grab a couple bags of chocolate chips and walnuts. They're on that bottom shelf over there. In fact, grab several. Thanksgiving is just around the corner and that means lots of baking. But cleaning the house comes

FREE BOOKS!

FREE GIFT!

PLAY THE "LUCKY 7" SLOT MACHINE GAME !

AND YOU CAN GET FREE BOOKS *PLUS* A FREE CUDDLY TEDDY BEAR!

NO COST! NO OBLIGATION TO BUY! NO PURCHASE NECESSARY!

PLAY "LUCKY 7" AND GET FIVE FREE GIFTS!

HOW TO PLAY:

1. With a coin, carefully scratch off the silver box at the right. Then check the claim chart to see what we have for you—FREE BOOKS and a gift—ALL YOURS! ALL FREE!

2. Send back this card and you'll receive brand-new Harlequin Romance® novels. These books have a cover price of $3.25 each, but they are yours to keep absolutely free.

3. There's no catch. You're under no obligation to buy anything. We charge nothing—ZERO—for your first shipment. And you don't have to make any minimum number of purchases—not even one!

4. The fact is thousands of readers enjoy receiving books by mail from the Harlequin Reader Service®. They like the convenience of home delivery...they like getting the best new novels months before they're available in stores...and they love our discount prices!

5. We hope that after receiving your free books you'll want to remain a subscriber. But the choice is yours—to continue or cancel, anytime at all! So why not take us up on our invitation, with no risk of any kind. You'll be glad you did!

You'll love this plush, cuddly Teddy Bear, an adorable accessory for your dressing table, bookcase or desk. Measuring 5½" tall, he's soft and brown and has a bright red ribbon around his neck—he's completely captivating! And he's yours absolutely free, when you accept this no-risk offer!

PLAY "LUCKY 7"

**Just scratch off the silver box with a coin.
Then check below to see the gifts you get.**

YES! I have scratched off the silver box. Please send me all the gifts for which I qualify. I understand I am under no obligation to purchase any books, as explained on the back and on the opposite page.

116 CIH A4VF
(U-H-R-11/96)

NAME

ADDRESS   APT.

CITY   STATE   ZIP

7 7 7	**WORTH FOUR FREE BOOKS PLUS A FREE CUDDLY TEDDY BEAR**
🍒 🍒 🍒	**WORTH THREE FREE BOOKS**
⬤ ⬤ ⬤	**WORTH TWO FREE BOOKS**
🔔 🔔 🍒	**WORTH ONE FREE BOOK**

DETACH AND MAIL CARD TODAY

THE HARLEQUIN READER SERVICE®: HERE'S HOW IT WORKS

Accepting free books places you under no obligation to buy anything. You may keep the books and gift and return the shipping statement marked "cancel". If you do not cancel, about a month later we'll send you 6 additional novels, and bill you just $2.67 each plus 25¢ delivery per book and applicable sales tax, if any.* That's the complete price—and compared to cover prices of $3.25 each—quite a bargain! You may cancel at any time, but if you choose to continue, every month we'll send you 6 more books, which you may either purchase at the discount price…or return to us and cancel your subscription.

*Terms and prices subject to change without notice. Sales tax applicable in N.Y.

If offer card is missing, write to: Harlequin Reader Service, 3010 Walden Ave., P.O. Box 1867, Buffalo, NY 14240-1867

BUSINESS REPLY MAIL
FIRST-CLASS MAIL   PERMIT NO. 717   BUFFALO, NY

POSTAGE WILL BE PAID BY ADDRESSEE

HARLEQUIN READER SERVICE
3010 WALDEN AVE
PO BOX 1867
BUFFALO NY 14240-9952

NO POSTAGE
NECESSARY
IF MAILED
IN THE
UNITED STATES

first, okay? I promised Jake. Cookies are a solid second."

Jake tried to ignore the annoying buzz of Peter's unending string of questions and stared moodily out the office window. Gradually he focused on the pickup parked across the street—a familiar-looking sleek, black, mud-spattered pickup. He frowned, suddenly realizing just why it looked so familiar. Dammit all! That sleek, black mud-splattered pickup was *his*.

"Hell and damnation," he swore. "She lied to me. That blasted woman promised she'd go to Two Forks and it was all a lie. I'm going to strangle her. I swear I will."

"What? What's she done?" Peter demanded.

"She's here. In town."

"So?"

"So, I told her to go to Two Forks, and she's deliberately disobeyed me."

Peter grinned. "I can't wait to meet this wife of yours. I'm really starting to like her."

"Go to hell, Bryant." Jake slapped his Stetson on his head and strode toward the door. "I'll finish with you later. Right now I've got to find my wife before she gets into trouble. Though knowing her, I'm way too late."

"Wait a minute. Jake! What about your grandfather's will? We need to set a court date. Wynne needs to—"

Jake stopped dead in his tracks and stomped back into the office. "I've changed my mind. I'm not having my wife stand up in open court and tell the whole of Chesterfield about our wedding night." He refused to turn such a private, soul-altering moment into fodder for Chesterfield's rumor mill. He couldn't do that to Wynne...or to himself. "You get Judge Graydon and Randolph to agree to a more private get-together. A...a dinner party or something, where we can all discuss it casual-like.''

''A dinner party,'' the lawyer repeated in disbelief. ''What's the plan, have her serve up the main course and say, 'Oh, by the way, Jake and I did it on our wedding night. Pass the salt and let's eat.'? I can just see that.''

Jake scowled. ''I won't allow Wynne to be embarrassed or humiliated in any way, shape or form. Understand? Can't the judge just ask how our wedding night went? She can tell him it was great and that'll be the end of it.''

''And was it? Great, I mean?''

Fury darkened Jake's face. ''If you weren't my lawyer, I'd knock your teeth down your throat.''

Peter grinned. ''Good thing I'm your lawyer then, isn't it? Wait a minute. One last question before you go.''

''What?''

''This is your temporary wife, right? The one who's leaving you once the terms of the will are met? The one you're not in love with?''

Jake scowled, pulling the brim of his hat low over his brow. ''That's three questions, Bryant, and not one of them is any of your business. Just arrange for the dinner. Got it?''

''Fine, but you'll have to talk to Wynne, explain what's expected of her.''

''I'll tell her.''

Maybe.

Or maybe he'd arrange for the judge to ask a few subtle questions over after-dinner coffee. He strode down the hall and out into the warm November sunlight, considering the matter. Wynne would never have to know the true purpose behind the get-together. He could keep it a secret. He'd just warn her that the judge was a nosy old man and she should humor him. It might work, if he planned carefully.

He shook his head in disgust.

Wynne's idealism must be rubbing off. Why else would he be casting himself in the role of her personal protector? When would he learn? He was the villain of the piece, dammit all, not the hero.

After signing the receipt for the groceries she'd purchased, Wynne offered Belle a cheerful farewell and pushed the loaded cart toward the exit. Before she'd reached it, a man planted himself square in front of her, blocking her path.

"Rumor has it you're married to Jake," he said by way of greeting. "Is that true?"

An unnatural silence descended on the crowded store and Wynne studied the man. Anger marred what might have been an attractive set of features and she wondered what she possibly could have done to antagonize him. "If you mean Jake Hondo, I'm his wife, yes," she admitted and offered her hand. "My name's Wynne." He pointedly ignored her gesture, instead hooking his thumbs in his belt loops and rocking back on his heels. She slowly dropped her arm.

"Jake only married you to get his hands on my inheritance," he announced, eyeing her belligerently.

She lifted her eyebrows in surprise. "*Your* inheritance?"

"Randolph, please," a sad-eyed woman behind him murmured, tugging on his arm. "Don't cause a scene."

He shook her off. "I'm Randolph Chesterfield and that ranch land he's after rightfully belongs to me."

"This land...it's his inheritance?"

"Only if he's properly wedded and bedded."

Wynne laughed. "Then there's no problem."

It was the wrong thing to say. Her comment only served to infuriate him. His hands closed into fists and he stepped closer, shoving her shopping cart to one side. "You can't know the man very well, or you wouldn't say that."

She lifted her chin, refusing to be intimidated. "I know Jake quite well and—"

"Then you know about the conditions of his grandfather's will." He shot the comment like a bullet. "You know he only married you to get my land."

"His land," she corrected with a sunny smile. "And of course I know why he married me. Not only is Jake an honest man, he's also the sweetest, kindest, most generous husband a woman could want. If it weren't for him, I wouldn't be able to keep my nephews." She wrapped her arms around Buster's and Chick's shoulders. "Why, as far as I'm concerned, he's an angel!"

Randolph's mouth opened and closed as he fought to digest her analysis of Jake's character. "He sure has you buffaloed," he said at last. "I don't know whether to pity you or congratulate him. But I'll give you fair warning. He doesn't give a plugged nickel for either you or those kids. You're nothing more to him than a means to an end. Once he gets what he's after, you and those kids will be out on your collective backsides."

"Randolph, please," the woman behind him said. "Let her be."

"Hush, Evie. I'm only speaking the truth. Someone ought to tell her about Jake—explain what a low-down, rotten snake he is before he hurts her or one of the kids."

"Uncle Jake's not a snake. And he wouldn't hurt us, neither. He loves us!" Buster shouted, his face turning red with indignation. "Don't you say anything bad about him or I'll kick you."

Wynne squeezed her nephew's shoulder. "It's all right, sweetheart. Mr. Chesterfield doesn't know Jake the way we do." She glared at Randolph. "You're wrong, mister. My husband is an honorable man, and one of these days he'll prove it to you. In the meantime, don't you say another nasty word about him to me or the children, or you'll regret it. Now, stand aside. It's time we left." She grabbed the cart and shoved it in his direction, deciding that if he didn't move out of the way, she'd run right over his toes.

With an exaggerated sweep of his arm, Randolph stepped back. "Don't let me keep you," he said as she stalked past. "But just out of curiosity... How much is he paying you to crawl into bed with him? It must be a bloody fortune."

A collective gasp ran through the store and Wynne felt her own anger skyrocket. But it was nothing compared to the fury that exploded across the countenance of the man lounging quietly in the doorway.

CHAPTER SIX

JAKE STRAIGHTENED, his eyes burning brighter than the fiery pits of hell. "I see you've met my wife, Chesterfield," he said, his voice all the more terrifying for its deadly control.

Startled, Randolph whipped around and blanched. "Hondo! I—"

Jake stepped closer, crowding the man against the wall. "You speak to her again without my permission and I'll permanently rearrange those pretty-boy features of yours. You got that?"

"Listen, Jake... I was just—"

"I didn't catch your answer." He grabbed a fistful of Randolph's shirt. "Are we communicatin' cousin? You don't speak to her. Hell, you don't even look at her. Understand?"

Sweat beaded Randolph's brow as he gave a tight-lipped nod.

Jake released his grip. "Smart answer. Because if you ever interfere in my business again, I'll put paid to your future existence. You have my personal guarantee." His attention switched to Wynne and he jerked his head toward the door. "Get goin'."

Without a word, she swept by. Buster followed in her wake, poking his tongue out at Randolph as he passed. Not to be outdone, Chick stopped and gave the man a swift kick in the shins before darting after his brother.

Jake's gaze swept the crowd of shoppers gathered to catch a glimpse of his wife. He wasn't surprised when few met his eyes. "Just so it's clear," he announced in a carrying voice. "I protect my own."

"No one doubts that," came Belle's dry retort. "But don't worry about Wynne. She made quite a hit the short time she was here."

Jake inclined his head. "Glad to hear it." Noticing Randolph's wife for the first time, he tipped his Stetson. "Always a pleasure, Evie."

"Damn you, Hondo. Leave her alone or I'll do some damage of my own," Randolph snarled, recovering a modicum of his aplomb. "You've got a wife now, remember? You don't need mine."

Tears sprang to Evie's gentle blue eyes and Jake instantly regretted turning his cousin's rage in her direction. He could handle it—she couldn't. But then, he hadn't expected Randolph's show of mettle. It had been a long time since he'd worked up the backbone to issue such a blatant challenge. Desperation must be riding him hard.

Jake inclined his head. "For the first time in your life, you're right, Chesterfield. I do have a wife now." He glanced over his shoulder at the gracefully swaying bottom disappearing down the sidewalk. "Our conversation can keep. She can't."

With that, he stalked from the store, his swift stride narrowing the gap between him and his troublesome wife. He caught up with her by the truck.

"What are you doing here, Wynne?" he asked as he helped dump bags of groceries into the bed of the pickup. "I thought I told you to go to Two Forks for supplies."

"You did."

Her back was to him and a cool breeze stirred the white-blond hair at her nape. A sharp pang of desire twisted his gut in knots. She was so delicate, so vulnerable. And so damned unpredictable. "Then why didn't you?" he demanded.

She glanced over her shoulder, her green eyes reflecting her surprise at his vehemence. "It was too far. I didn't think I could make it."

"What do you mean...couldn't make it?"

"It's the three pedals," Buster offered. "I tried to help, but she's not very good at it."

"Three—" Understanding dawned. "You don't know how to drive a stick shift?" he questioned ominously.

"I do...in theory. I'm just not so great at the 'in practice' part," she confessed.

He swallowed the multitude of retorts that leapt to his tongue. "Get in the truck," he instructed. "I'll follow you home."

Chick sighed.

Buster rolled his eyes and groaned. "Uh-oh."

Jake glared. "What's wrong now?"

"I don't do reverse," she explained.

"You don't—" He bit off an exclamation. "But you *can* go forward, correct?"

She grinned. "Well enough to have gotten us here."

"Well enough to get you back home again, too?"

"I think so."

He yanked open the cab door. "Stand on the sidewalk. I'll back the truck out."

Buster tugged on Wynne's arm. "Uncle Jake sounds funny again," he whispered. "Like when he was in the store."

"I think that means he's annoyed," she whispered back.

"I'm not annoyed." Jake corrected her grimly. "I'm mad enough to spit nails. Now go stand on that sidewalk like I told you."

Silently they did as he asked. Starting the engine with a roar, he spun out of the parking space and left the pickup idling in the middle of the street. "Hop in and start for home," he called to Wynne. "I'll be right on your tail."

The three climbed into the truck. With an earsplitting grinding of gears, Wynne popped the clutch into first and coughed her way down the road. Jake winced. His mechanic was going to love her. At a transmission a month, Billy Dee would soon be able to afford that Hummer he'd been eyeing. Shaking his head in disgust, Jake climbed into an ancient Jeep and planted his front bumper inches off her back one. The first time she stalled the engine, he almost rear-ended her. After that, he kept a respectable distance between them.

Ten minutes later they reached the driveway to Lost Trail. It took three tries for her to find the right gear and keep the engine running long enough to make the turn. Jake released a gusty sigh. He had a horrible feeling this was only the beginning of his tribulations with his adorable wife. Unfortunately he had a tough time working up any real irritation with her—especially after her spirited defense of him in the general store.

Dusty emerged from the barn to greet them as they pulled into the yard. He eyed Wynne and the children with trepidation. "That her?" he questioned, poking his head in the open window of the Jeep. "Where'd the kids come from? Don't remember you sayin' anything about kids."

"I told you my wife packed a few surprises. They're just one of them. Come on and I'll introduce you."

Dusty held up his hands and started backing toward the barn. "That's not necessary. Any ol' time will do. Next week. Next month. How 'bout while they're packing to leave?"

Jake shook his head. "Not a chance. You'll meet them now. That way you can keep an eye on the kids while I teach Wynne how to drive a stick."

"I'm no baby-sitter," Dusty protested.

"Yeah? Well, you're not much of a foreman, either. But I don't see that that's ever stopped you from collecting the wages of one. Now shut your yap and come on." A sudden thought occurred and he swiveled to glare a warning. "And don't spit on her."

Wynne turned her attention from the endless expanse of pastureland flying by the truck window and glanced at Jake. "I appreciate your teaching me to drive the truck."

"You should have told me you'd never driven a standard transmission before."

She shrugged. "I didn't notice it was standard until we were ready to go shopping."

"Once you did notice, you should have waited until I returned. You could have caused an accident."

Silence descended again and she twirled her wedding band around her finger, scrambling for something else to say. "The people of Chesterfield are really nice," she volunteered. "Belle sure does have a busy store. I guess that's why you wanted me to go to Two Forks, right? Because it isn't as crowded there?"

"Wrong. Belle's place was so packed because word spread that a Mrs. Jake Hondo had wandered in to do her shopping. They were all curious to meet the woman brave enough to take me on." A muscle worked in his jaw. "I wanted you to go to Two Forks to avoid all those nice, curious people. In particular, I'd hoped to avoid Randolph."

She blinked. "Oh. Well, except for him, Chesterfield's an awfully friendly town. I probably met just about everyone. What a wonderful place to celebrate the holidays." She slanted him another look. "I wonder why Randolph took such a dislike to me."

"I believe he explained that."

"Then he wasn't lying about the inheritance?"

"No."

Another thought occurred to her. "You must have been standing there a long time to have heard all that."

"Long enough."

"Jake—"

His hands tightened on the steering wheel. "Although he denies the relationship, Randolph's my cousin—a distant cousin, but a cousin nonetheless. Is that what you wanted to know?"

"Why?"

He sighed. "Why what?"

"Why does he deny the relationship?"

"Because my father, Weston Chesterfield the third, wasn't married to my mother. Ours is an accidental connection, not a legitimate one and he resents it like hell. I may carry the blood of a Chesterfield, but I'm not one according to the law."

"But that's not the only reason he resents you," she guessed.

"No. His anger intensified when my grandfather left his ranch to me—with one small condition, that is."

"Marriage?"

"You got it."

"And if you hadn't married?"

"The ranch would have gone to Randolph."

"But why would your grandfather add such an odd provision?" she asked. "Why force you to marry?"

"Because he was a meddling old fool who wanted great-grandchildren."

"But—"

"This discussion is over." He spun onto a gravel shoulder beneath a huge cottonwood tree and switched off the ignition. Open ranch land stretched in all directions. "It's your turn to drive."

Wisely abandoning her previous line of questioning, she asked, "Where are we?"

"Close to the north end of my property. No one ever comes this way except my men, and they're several clips west of here working my grandfather's spread. We should have this stretch of road all to ourselves."

"No one to run into?" she teased.

He didn't deny it. "It'll be a hell of a lot safer teaching you here than on the road into Chesterfield, that's for sure."

"Trying to mitigate damages?" she asked wryly.

"Somebody better. My insurance coverage only goes so far. You ready?"

To her surprise, instead of exiting the vehicle, he slid over until they were joined hip to thigh. In the next instant, he'd pulled her onto his lap, cradling her in his arms.

"I'm not complaining, you understand," she said, snuggling deeper into his embrace. "But I thought you were going to teach me to drive a stick shift."

"I am."

She grinned. "I might find it a little difficult learning while sitting like this."

"Fat lot you know. I think this is a perfect learning position."

"But I can't reach the clutch from here." She stuck out her foot to demonstrate.

"You don't need to reach it. You already know where all the various parts are. It's how they work together that you need to learn."

She swallowed. "We're still talking about driving, right?" she asked in a husky voice.

He lifted a sooty eyebrow. "What else would we be talking about?"

She had no intention of answering that one. "Maybe we should get started," she murmured.

"Fine. Let's talk about first gear." He settled her more comfortably on his lap, his warm breath caressing her mouth. "First gear is where you start off. It's sort of like ... well ... like a first kiss."

"A kiss."

"A first kiss," he said, correcting her.

She tilted her head to one side and frowned. "There's a difference?"

"You better believe it. If you're smart and want to keep everything running smoothly, you ease into a first kiss, slow and gentle. Like this." His mouth brushed hers, lingering, probing.

Her eyes drifted closed. "Slow and gentle," she managed to repeat.

"That's right. If you begin with a light, easy touch, you'll slip right into gear without any resistance." His tongue eased past her lips, caressing the softness inside. "See?"

She moaned. "I think so. Maybe we better make sure. Why don't you show me again?"

He didn't need any further prompting, but gave her a thorough grounding in the complexities of first gear. "I think we're moving toward second," he murmured after several minutes.

"How do you know?"

"The closer you get, the more the engine hums. When it starts to strain, it's a warning that first isn't getting the job done. Then you drop into the next gear."

"Second, right?" She tilted back her head, giving him access to the hollow at the base of her neck.

"Right." His mouth followed the length of her throat. "Now if first is a kiss, second is a touch." His hand slid from her shoulder downward. "It's just a tease, really. A prelude to more exciting things to come."

She shivered beneath his playful fingers. "Does it last long?"

"Depends on where you are." He fumbled with the buttons of her blouse. "And what sort of impediments are in your way. If your progress is interrupted, you might even have to go back to first.''

''And if there aren't any?'' The edges of her shirt fell open. ''Impediments, I mean?''

He stroked his index finger along the line of her bra. ''You hit the gas to get things moving faster. When the engine starts to strain again, then you push for third.''

It was an effort to breathe. ''What's third like?''

''Third is a bolder caress.''

She licked her lips. ''How bold?''

He unhooked the front of her bra and parted the silky cups. ''This bold.'' He demonstrated and her breath stopped completely. ''You're picking up speed, moving faster down the road. The tempo accelerates with third.''

''I remember.'' She shuddered beneath his touch, burying her face in his shoulder. ''But I never went past third. I was afraid to go any faster.''

''Then we'll shift into fourth together.'' He turned her so she faced him, her knees hugging his hips, his corded thigh muscles like taut ropes beneath her bottom. ''Fourth is all the way, sweetpea. There's no turning back. It's a hard, fast ride with the engine wide open. It feels great. And for a while you think it's right where you should be. Where you belong.''

His hands had slipped to places better suited to the velvet darkness of a moonlit night. The breath sobbed from her lungs. Even as she surged toward some unobtainable peak, she knew she'd never reach it. Not here. Not now. Her fingers dug into his shoulders. ''It's not enough!''

''That's when you shift into fifth.'' He pulled her tight against him so every move he made, every breath he took was echoed by her own body. ''Fifth is that final release. Fifth takes you to the end of the road.''

She squeezed her eyes closed, his scent filling her nostrils, his breath hot against her ear, his taste sweetening her tongue. She was afraid to move, afraid to break the connection pulsing between them. "And after fifth?" Her words were labored, her voice nearly inaudible.

"There's nowhere else to go after that and only one possible option."

"What option?"

His mouth sought hers, his tongue breaching her lips in a soft, gentle caress. "You can throw it into reverse and start all over again."

"Oh, yes!" The words escaped on a sigh. "Take me for another ride."

"What the hell is going on?" Jake came out of the truck in one fluid motion. Dusty, Buster and Chick stood in a row, all three scuffing dirt with their toes and avoiding his eyes. "I just passed Mad Dog burning up the field a mile north of here. How did he get out?"

No one said a word.

"My prize stallion is in the same pasture as my prize bull and you three have nothing to say? What do you suppose the odds are that one or both of my animals will end up as hamburger meat on tonight's dinner table?" He glared from one set of guilty features to the next, sexual frustration erupting into anger. "Well? Who's gonna start talkin' first?"

Dusty cleared his throat. "Guess that's me. It was...ah...it was an accident."

Jake's eyebrows arched skyward. "Mad Dog escaped out of a padlocked stall by accident? How'd he manage that, sprout wings?"

Wynne climbed from the truck and joined Jake. "Buster? You were asked a question. What happened?"

Buster raised tear-filled eyes. "I'm sorry, Uncle Jake. I just wanted to show Chick how to ride a horse."

The color bleached from Jake's face and he fought to keep his knees from buckling. "You let that horse out? *You*?"

Buster nodded miserably. "I saw where the key was hanging and thought I'd see if your horse would let me ride him. He was real sweet. He followed me outside just like a puppy dog."

"That...that *puppy dog* is the meanest son of a b—gun on this ranch. If he didn't sire such prize-winning offspring, I'd put a quick end to his sorry existence. You could have been—" He closed his eyes, fighting not to think about the "could-have-beens."

Chick released a hiccuping sob and launched himself at Jake's knees, nearly toppling him.

"It was my fault, boss," Dusty muttered. "When I saw the kid with Mad Dog, I sort of lost it. I started hollerin' and that crazy hoss rolled back his eyes and kicked up his heels. I gotta confess, though. The kid has real good reflexes. He rolled clear of Mad Dog's shenanigans, grabbed his little brother by the scruff of the neck and skedaddled onto the porch."

Jake's hands balled into fists. "I thought I asked you to watch them, Dusty. You call this watching them?"

"I only turned my back for a minute. I swear. Was showin' them around, 'splaining how stuff works and the next thing I know, they took off on me."

"Oh, Buster," Wynne said with a sigh. "You know better than to disappear without telling the person in charge where you're going. You also know better than to touch someone else's property without permission."

"And if he didn't before, he's sure going to learn now," Jake stated in no uncertain terms. He stabbed a finger first at Buster and then at Chick. "Both of you. Get to the barn and wait for me."

"What are you going to do to them?" Wynne asked apprehensively.

"We're going to have a man-to-man talk. And if they're lucky they'll be able to sit down sometime next week." He didn't wait for a response, but turned to Dusty. "As for you... If you want to keep your job, not to mention your hide, you'll round up the men and go corral that horse."

"Yessir, boss. I'll get right on it," he said and raced toward the Jeep as fast as his stubby legs would take him.

"Jake?"

Wynne touched his arm and he deliberately kept his back to her. If he looked at her, he'd never be able to discipline the boys. One glimpse of her huge, pleading eyes and all his good intentions would melt like ice beneath a noonday sun. "What is it?"

"Make sure they understand what they did wrong. Otherwise they'll never learn."

It took him a minute to digest her words. "What did you say?" he whispered.

"A ranch in Texas is a lot different than an apartment in Maryland. I don't think they quite realize that yet."

Slowly he turned to look at her and the trust he read in her calm expression left him fighting for control. "You're not afraid I'll hurt them?" he questioned roughly.

She actually laughed. "Don't be ridiculous. I know you'd never do that, despite what Randolph said. Buster shouldn't have touched Mad Dog. And as you said, if he doesn't realize it now, he will as soon as you speak to him."

He cleared his throat. "I won't be long."

"There's no hurry," she replied. "I'll start dinner while you deal with the boys."

He couldn't answer. Instead he nodded and headed for the barn. The boys were waiting just inside the door. Buster stood in front of his brother, his expression one of stoic resolve. The phrase "taking it like a man" leapt to mind and Jake studied them in silence, waiting. Buster broke first.

"We're sorry for what we did, Uncle Jake. And it won't never happen again. We promise."

Chick peeked apprehensively around his brother and nodded, before popping his thumb into his mouth and sucking furiously.

Jake inclined his head. "That's good to know. Because if I can't trust your word, I'll have to restrict you to the house instead of having you help around the ranch." Surprise warred with exhilaration on their expressive faces.

"Really? You mean it? We can help you?"

"I wouldn't have said it if I hadn't meant it."

"We promise!" Buster stated fervently. "We'll do everything you say."

Chick tugged on his brother's arm and whispered something.

"Okay, I'll ask." Buster glanced at Jake. "You want both of us to help, right?"

"Yep. A ranch this size needs every pair of hands available." He gave Buster a stern look. "But there's a lot of dangerous animals and equipment on a ranch. One thoughtless mistake can get you seriously hurt—like with Mad Dog. I know you wouldn't want Chick injured through your carelessness."

"No, sir," came the somber reply.

"That means you can't do anything without asking permission first. You got that?"

"Got it."

Chick gave a decisive nod of agreement.

"Okay. The only problem is . . . Your little stunt today has caused Dusty and my men a lot of extra work, which means they're going to have trouble getting all their chores done."

Buster didn't hesitate. "Maybe we could do some of those chores."

Jake pretended to consider. "You know, I think that's an excellent way to make amends." He hooked a thumb toward a pair of pitchforks propped in the corner of the barn. "Let's see how good you are at pitching hay." He watched in satisfaction as the boys scrambled to obey. A little hard work and they'd be too worn-out to get into any more mischief. He hoped.

Which just left Wynne. He rubbed a hand across his jaw and grinned. That shouldn't be much of a problem, either. If he put his mind to it, he didn't doubt he could think of one or two activities to keep her occupied. Like reviewing what she'd learned about driving a stick shift. Only this time, he'd make sure they didn't just talk about fifth gear.

He'd make sure they experienced it, as well.

CHAPTER SEVEN

JAKE SAT at his grandfather's desk and stared at the bills and correspondence littering the oak surface. Just over a week had passed since he'd returned home and a veritable mountain of work had piled up. He'd hoped by coming to the Chesterfield ranch he'd find the peace and quiet to accomplish it. No runaway horses. No grouchy foreman. No hero-worshiping kids. And no starry-eyed wife who thought the sun rose and set at her husband's behest.

But instead of settling down to business, he found himself gazing off into space, picturing an impish smile, winter-white hair and impassioned green eyes. In the past week he'd developed an uncontrollable need to steal Wynne away as frequently as possible and review the finer points of driving a standard transmission. Worse, when he wasn't preoccupied with his wife, his mind turned to what new activity he'd introduce to the boys and how he might wheedle one, tiny word out of Chick.

The phone at his elbow rang and he snatched it up with relief—anything to block such appealing, impossible daydreams. "Hondo."

"Thought I might find you there," Peter's satisfied voice echoed down the line. "I just spoke to Judge Graydon. He approved the dinner party."

"Glad to hear it."

"I don't think he liked the idea of a public hearing, either. As for a date... He's available Saturday night. Randolph, needless to say, is protesting for all he's worth.

116

Not that it's done a lick of good. Graydon supports you in this instance."

"I assume my cousin has to be there," Jake stated with a marked lack of enthusiasm.

"'Fraid so. I did suggest he bring Evie. I'm hoping she'll help control that temper of his."

"Not likely. But I trust you impressed on him the importance of keeping his mouth shut around my wife."

"I did, and I sincerely doubt he'll start any trouble. I think the incident at Belle's was a sufficient deterrent. He won't be interested in a repeat performance."

"Let's hope you're right."

"So, that just leaves Wynne. I assume you've talked to her? She knows what to expect?"

"I'll deal with that end of things, you worry about the legalities."

"Fine." There was a significant pause. "I'm curious to meet her, considering the impression she's made around here. People in town have been talking about little else. Seems everyone has a story involving her."

"Involving her how?" Jake demanded.

"You know... Her contributions to charity, how she visits the shut-ins, the way she cares for her nephews, her nonstop defense of you." Peter chuckled. "Woe betide anyone who speaks ill of her husband. She lets them have it with both barrels."

"Does she?" Jake murmured, grinning.

"Sure does. When the time comes, you'll have to fight off her suitors with a stick."

"When the time comes?" Jake's brows drew together, his grin dying a rapid death. "What time? And what suitors? What the hell are you talking about?"

There was an uncomfortable silence. Then Peter admitted, "Randolph's continued to spread the rumor around town that your marriage is a pretense. That as soon as the judge gives his final approval, you'll divorce her. Though in all honesty, it's not much of a rumor, is it?"

"The length of my marriage is nobody's business but mine."

"And Wynne's," Peter retorted coolly. "Anyway... Every bachelor within sixty miles who's exchanged so much as a word with her, is hot to cozy up to the soon-to-be ex-Mrs. Hondo. They all think she'd make a perfect wife. I probably would, too, if I'd ever met her."

Jake's hand closed into a white-knuckle fist. The soon-to-be ex-Mrs. Hondo? *Ex*-Mrs. Hondo? "You so much as look at her funny," he snarled, "and not only will you be my *ex*-lawyer, you'll also be my *ex*-friend carrying around a handful of *ex*-teeth."

He banged down the phone and thrust back his chair. Damn Peter for stirring up such disturbing images. The problem was... He was probably right. Most men would consider Wynne the answer to their dreams, kids and all. If she'd come to Chesterfield looking for a husband, instead of to the Montagues' ball, she'd have had potential husbands lined up and begging for her hand. And they wouldn't have been interested in any temporary arrangement, either. They'd have been every bit as intent as Wynne on having a happily-ever-after marriage.

Unable to contain his restlessness, Jake wandered through his grandfather's ranch house, picking up the occasional knickknack before setting it back in place. As reluctant as he was to admit it, he loved the ranch almost as much as he'd loved his grandfather. But it was a love mixed with anger and resentment, stirring to life demons better left undisturbed. Chesterfield Ranch represented all he'd been denied as a child. Hell, he'd never stepped foot inside the house proper until he was practically an adult. And then—when it was far too late—he'd been offered it all.

It was a beautiful place, he reluctantly conceded, one that cried out for a family. His grandfather had often said that it would never be a true home without the ring of youthful voices bouncing off its high, sweeping ceilings. For the first time, Jake understood what that meant.

The house seemed to be holding its breath, its walls achingly empty of the plethora of childish artwork it needed to accent the knotty juniper trim. The air smelled stale and unused without the scent of cookies baking in the kitchen or the light tantalizing fragrance of a woman's perfume. And the rooms were too neat—no cookbooks left in an open pile on the table, no toys scattered haphazardly across the carpet, no woman's accessories cluttering the bathroom. If he closed his eyes, he could almost picture how it would react to Wynne and the boys.

He found the image all too appealing.

With a muttered exclamation, he returned to the office and snatched his Stetson off the hat rack. Not only was he a fool, but he was also the grandson of a fool. And if he didn't get out of here right now, he'd do something stupid. Like pack up Wynne and the boys and turn this house into the home it was meant to be.

"Wynne? You there?" Jake yanked off his muddy boots—something he'd never have done until a week ago—and opened the door to the kitchen. "Elf?"

"Look out, Jake!" he heard her panicked shout. "Don't come in."

"Why not?" Already in the room, he stared at Wynne in disbelief. "What the hell are you doing on the counter?"

Buster peeked down from the top of the refrigerator. "Hey there, Uncle Jake."

He stared from one to the other. "Mind telling me what's going on?"

A cupboard door swung open and from his curled-up perch on the shelf, Chick pointed toward a splash of sunlight on the floor.

Jake turned to look, then jumped back, cutting loose with a blistering expletive.

"I did try to warn you," Wynne said meekly.

"Next time forget all the 'look out' and 'don't come in' stuff and just scream, 'snake.' Trust me, I'll get the message." He stared at the reptile coiled on the floor and let out a long, low whistle. "That has got to be the biggest damn—darn rattler I've ever seen in my life."

"We weren't certain that's what it was, but we didn't want to take any chances."

"Smart move, sweetheart." He shot them a quick look, tension gripping him. "Everybody all right? Anyone bit?"

"We're fine," Wynne reassured.

"Chick needs to pee real bad," Buster chimed in. "I thought about havin' him wet down the snake, but figured it would only make the thing madder. Maybe mad enough to slither up here and get even."

Jake fought to keep a straight face. "I appreciate your restraint."

As though tired of being left out of the conversation, the snake swung its spade-shaped head in his direction, its tail quivering an ominous warning. Jake froze, knowing better than to make any sudden moves.

"Would you mind putting it outside?" Wynne requested nervously.

"Would I mind—" He eyed the distance between him and the snake. "No, sweetpea. I wouldn't mind. As a matter of fact, I'll get right on it." Deciding he was far enough away to avoid an unexpected strike, he backed slowly toward the mudroom. Scooping up his boots, he donned them with due speed.

He poked his head around the door. "Care to explain how you came to be entertaining a diamondback?"

"It wasn't by choice, believe me. It must have been hibernating in the woodbox by the stove. We were going to try baking cookies on the fire-burner and I opened the box to get some wood and—"

"It's a wood-burner and I get the picture." His shut his eyes. In fact, it was all too vivid a picture, almost crippling in its impact. It was also an image he'd have to hold at bay if he were to be of any use. "Listen to me, Wynne. I need to get to the den and since I don't think our friend here is going to let me by without payin' a stiff penalty, I'll have to circle around. I'll be back as quick as I can. Stay put, okay?"

"No worries there," Wynne replied, attempting a smile.

Not wasting another minute, he exited through the mudroom and ran like hell for the front of the house. In thirty seconds flat, he'd beat a path to the den, had the gun case unlocked and his rifle loaded. Ramming home the shell, he headed for the kitchen. At the doorway, he paused, checking cautiously for the snake. It hadn't moved, but lay coiled in the sunlight, warming itself.

"All of you, turn around and don't look," he ordered.

"What are you going to do with the gun?" Wynne asked apprehensively.

"What do you think? I'm going to blow that critter to kingdom come."

"Here?" she questioned, appalled. "In the kitchen?"

"Right here and right now." He shouldered the rifle. "Close your eyes. It's gonna be messy."

"Jake, no. You can't."

He sighted along the barrel. "What do you mean I can't? I'll have you know I'm a dead shot."

She lowered her voice. "Not in front of the children, you aren't."

"Why not?" Buster demanded. "We want to see Uncle Jake blow the snake to kingdom come."

Chick nodded, his powder-blue eyes gleaming with bloodthirsty enthusiasm. He popped his thumb from his mouth and took aim with his index finger. "*Pkkkww.*"

Wynne stared at him in delight. "Chick! You spoke."

Buster made a sound of disgust. "*Pkkkww* isn't a word. It's a noise. You know, like a gun blast."

"Oh." She looked crestfallen for an instant, then brightened. "That's okay, Chick," she said with an encouraging smile. "You'll talk when you're good and ready."

"Excuse me, but could we *please* focus on the problem at hand?" Jake interrupted, an exasperated edge to his voice.

She frowned. "Right. The snake. I'd really rather you not shoot it in the house. In fact . . . I'm not sure I want it shot, period." She gazed hopefully at Jake. "Can't we just move it someplace else?"

He lowered his rifle. "You don't have a clue, do you?" He pointed. "For your information, that snake is a western diamondback. It's the second most venomous reptile in the U.S. Know what that means?"

Eyes enormous, Wynne shook her head.

"It means that this snake's gonna meet its maker and I'm the one who's sending it there. And if I find any of its brothers, sisters or cousins hanging around, they'll join 'im in snake heaven." He shook his head in disbelief. "Why the hell—damn!—*heck* am I even standing here discussing this, when I should be taking care of business?"

"But—"

"Forget it," he said flatly. "Do you really want to risk one of the kids getting bit? Because that's what could happen if I don't kill it."

"Of course I don't want the boys put at risk. But... Can't you kill it outside?"

"How do you expect me to get it there? Say 'Hey, pardner, would you mind slitherin' outside so we can discuss this problem man-to-reptile?'"

"You don't have to be sarcastic."

Dusty burst through the mudroom door. "What's all the excitement?" he demanded, panting for breath. "Saw you running like your britches were afire." Spotting the snake, he squawked and scrambled backward.

Apparently Dusty's arrival was one human too many. With a furious shake of its tail, the rattler slithered toward him.

"What the hell are you waiting for, boss?" Dusty shouted. "Shoot the sucker!"

"Sorry, old friend. My wife won't let me. And watch your language in front of the boys."

"This ain't funny, Jake. Come on! Shoulder that blowpipe and let 'er rip, will ya?"

"Not unless Wynne agrees."

"I'm runnin' short of options here," Dusty bellowed as the rattler rapidly closed the distance between them. "What do you want me to do? Spit on the dang thing? Fire, I say. Fire!"

"Wynne?"

"*Boss*!"

"Okay! Shoot it! Shoot it!" Wynne yelped, tumbling off the counter.

The snake swung in her direction, preparing to strike. It was the last move it ever made.

The rifle blast practically deafened them. Peeking through her fingers, Wynne saw Dusty flat on his back, a cloud of dust and debris hanging over him. The snake lay in a small crater nearby, unmoving.

She fought for breath. "Dusty." His name escaped in a panicked whisper. "Oh, no. What have I done? Dusty, speak to me. Are you bit? Shot? What's wrong?"

"He passed out," Jake informed her dryly. "Too much excitement, I guess."

With a groan, the foreman sat up and looked around. Spying the dead snake, his face split into a wide grin. "Looks like I got me a new belt. Maybe a hatband, too." He picked up the snake by its tail and glanced at Wynne, offering generously, "Want the rattle for a key chain?"

Jake didn't give her a chance to reply, but dropped his rifle onto the table and literally snatched her off the floor, enfolding her in a fierce embrace. "You scared the life out of me, you know that?" he muttered. "I can't leave you alone for five seconds without your getting into some scrape or another."

She wrapped her arms around his waist, giving him a reassuring hug. His heart pounded against her cheek, his rapid breath stirring the hair at her temple. A familiar lethargy stole over her, leaving her deaf and blind to everything but Jake. It was always this way when he touched her and she couldn't help but wonder if he felt the same. "Maybe next time you'd better just shoot it," she offered generously.

"Instead of listening to my wife? Thanks. I'll do that." He glanced at the boys. "Hop down. The show's over."

"That was cool!" Buster enthused. "Will you teach me how to use a gun like that?"

"Absolutely not," Wynne answered, reluctantly leaving Jake's arms.

"You'll be far too busy packing," he added smoothly.

"Packing?" All four turned to stare at him.

He folded his arms across his chest, his chin set at a familiarly stubborn angle. "It's not safe at Lost Trail. So, we're moving over to my grandfather's ranch."

Dusty's jaw dropped. "Have you lost your mind?" he asked. "You're movin' them over to the Chesterfield spread because of one little ol' snake?"

"Yes."

"What for? That diamondback happens to be the most common in the whole gol' dern state of Texas. It's not like you can put up No Trespassing signs to keep it off Chesterfield property, you know."

"We're moving and that's final." Jake glared at his foreman, daring him to argue further. "Any other objections?"

Wynne cleared her throat. "What about my cookies?"

He stared at her blankly. "Come again?"

"We have cookies to bake for Mrs. McCracken." She gestured toward a large ceramic bowl sitting on the table. "I have the dough ready and everything."

Jake frowned. "Who's Mrs. McCracken?"

"You know," Dusty said. "That cranky ol' bitty who lives next to the schoolhouse. Enjoys poor health. Always has some ailment or other to moan about."

"She's laid up with sciatica, I saw a notice at Belle's. So I thought the boys and I could take a few things over to her. I'm sure she'd enjoy the company."

"You're jes a regular ol' Polly—butter wouldn't melt in her mouth—anna, ain't you?" Dusty muttered. "Cookies for this charity, brownies for that. Cakes for the poor little orphans."

Wynne looked alarmed. "What orphans? I didn't hear about them."

"There aren't any orphans, ya dang..." Dusty yanked his hat so low it hid half his face. "Never mind."

She tilted her head to one side, a sudden thought occurring to her. "You know, I think I made way too large a batch. I just might have a few cookies left over. I don't suppose..." She heaved a sigh. "No, I guess not."

Dusty clutched the snake to his chest, a greedy expression creeping across his wrinkled countenance. "Don't suppose, what?"

"That you and the men might like some." She gave him an innocent look. "Or don't cowboys eat cookies?"

Dusty scowled, clearly fighting a battle between pride and stomach. "Wouldn't want to hurt your feelings by refusin'," he said at last. "I guess we could get rid of them if nobody else will."

"I'd appreciate that," she said, deciding then and there to have extra cookies available on a regular basis. "Oh! I almost forgot." Crossing to the ceramic bowl, she fished out her wedding ring and slipped it back on her finger. She peeked over at Jake. "That snake distracted me so badly, I'd almost forgotten it had fallen off."

"We should have that sized before you really lose it." He turned to scowl at the woodbox. "As for your cookies... Load your dough into the truck. You can bake them over at my grandfather's." That should help the ranch house smell like a home—that and Wynne's heady brand of scent. "Let's move, people. We have work to do."

Dusty shook his head, muttering, "First we live here for a spell. Then we up and move to Mr. Chesterfield's place when he got hisself sick. Then we move ev'rbody to Lost Trail 'cause you're gettin' married. Now we're goin' back again after jes ten bitty days." He stomped toward the door. "I wish you'd make up your blasted mind, Boss. I'm gettin' dizzy."

The shift from Lost Trail to the Chesterfield ranch took longer than anticipated, the move not finalized until the day of the dinner party. Wynne didn't bother unpacking her personal possessions, instead focusing on getting ready for the evening. Carrying a stack of plates into the dining room, she placed them on the sideboard and glanced around in satisfaction. The table could seat a dozen people, which was more than adequate for their plans. It would also be perfect for Thanksgiving.

"Hello? Anybody home?" A man carrying a huge bouquet of flowers appeared in the doorway, stopping dead at the sight of her. "You're Wynne?" he demanded. "Jake's wife?"

"That's right," she confirmed, wondering why he found her identity so amazing. "And you're...?"

"Sorry." Recovering swiftly, he offered an engaging grin. "Peter Bryant, Jake's lawyer and occasional friend. I didn't mean to stare, but you aren't quite what I expected. I didn't know Jake had such good taste."

"It's a pleasure to meet you." She tilted her head to one side. "Why occasional?"

"Pardon?"

"You said, 'occasional friend.' Why?"

"I have this annoying habit of ticking him off," he confided.

Her mouth twitched. "And when that happens you're not his friend anymore?"

"So he claims."

She eyed the flowers. "Are those for me?"

"Oh, right." He held them out. "It's a welcome to the neighborhood gift. A little late, I'm afraid. But they're actually just an excuse to meet you before dinner tonight."

Wynne laughed. "You didn't need an excuse. And you certainly don't need flowers. You're welcome anytime."

"In all honesty, I wish I could claim I'd brought them out of the goodness of my heart. But the truth is I wanted to make sure we're ready for tonight."

She shot him a startled glance. Was this evening more important than she'd realized? "I think we are. Everything's sort of hit at once—the move, the dinner party. Did you know that this will be our first night staying here?"

"Jake mentioned something to that effect. I couldn't believe it when he said he planned to move you all over here." Before she could ask why, he added, "But you haven't answered my question."

"About whether I'm ready for tonight?" She gestured toward the sideboard. "I'm setting the table right now. The meal won't take anytime to put together and—"

"The house looks beautiful, and I'm sure dinner will be perfect," he interrupted, a small frown furrowing his brow. "I guess what I really meant to ask was—how you're doing. You're not worried about the real reason for tonight's gathering, are you?"

"The real reason..." She stilled, something in his tone warning her to tread cautiously. "Would you care for a cup of coffee?" she offered.

"And some of those cookies I've heard so much about?" he suggested with boyish eagerness.

She managed a smile. "They certainly have helped cement my relationship with Dusty. It's amazing what a man will do for a plateful of cookies."

"They must be some cookies." He followed her into the kitchen. Opening a cupboard with obvious familiarity, he removed two mugs and filled them with the coffee she'd just finished brewing. "How do you take it?"

"With milk and sugar."

He poked his head in the refrigerator and removed the carton of milk. "I assume Jake's spoken to you about tonight?"

"Sure." She loaded up a plate with cookies and joined him at the table. "I was a bit surprised to hear Randolph is coming."

Peter helped himself to an oatmeal raisin. "He wouldn't miss it for the world. He still lives in hope that he can do Jake out of his inheritance." He waved the cookie at her. "Hey, these are great. No wonder Dusty's been jumping through hoops."

"Thanks. So long as I keep the cookie jar filled, we're the best of friends." She hesitated, then asked, "I don't understand something. Jake and I are legally married, right? So why would Randolph think he could win at this late stage?"

"Because Judge Graydon hasn't recognized the marriage. He can't until after he talks to you tonight and confirms that you... That you and Jake... You know." He snagged another cookie. "I thought Jake explained all this."

She buried her nose in the coffee cup, suddenly aware that there was a whole lot she didn't understand. "It must have slipped my mind."

"If there weren't so much at stake, it would be funny. Before Jake married you, it was all cut-and-dried. He'd pick out a plain, practical, levelheaded woman, marry her and then march her into court."

"Practical? No wonder you were surprised when we first met," she murmured.

"You don't exactly fit the criteria," he admitted, before hastening to add, "Not that it matters. The only vital requirement was that his wife be willing to stand up in front of the judge and half the world and make the necessary statement. But ever since he brought you home, he's been all hot and bothered about fulfilling this particular condition."

What condition? And what statement? She wished she could come right out and ask. But she didn't dare. Peter obviously assumed Jake had explained it all to her. Which prompted yet another question: *Why hadn't he?*

"You said Jake was concerned about this part of the will. Why?"

"He doesn't want you embarrassed. Told me to get the judge to agree to something more private." Peter shrugged awkwardly. "At least you won't have to stand up in court and inform the whole of Chesterfield that you consummated the marriage. Although doing it over dinner is bad enough, I suppose."

She paled, her mug clattering against the table. "I have to—"

"Unbelievable isn't it?" Peter shook his head. "Mr. Chesterfield sure was a crazy ol' coot. But he was desperate to have Jake married in every sense of the word."

"Why?" she asked again.

Peter shifted uncomfortably. "You'll have to ask Jake about that." He finished his coffee and stood, snitching an extra couple of cookies. "Well, sorry to eat and run. But as I said, I just needed to confirm that everything's set."

"I appreciate your stopping by." More than he'd ever know.

"Thanks for your hospitality. I'll see you later tonight."

For the hour following Peter's departure, Wynne finished setting the dining-room table, turning their conversation over in her mind as she did so. She kept coming back to the same concern. *Why hadn't Jake told her what to expect?* Was he just going to drop it on her right before their guests arrived? It didn't make sense.

By midafternoon, everything was ready. The silverware shone, she'd polished the fine cherrywood table to a lustrous finish and the flowers Peter had given her were arranged in a silver bowl as a centerpiece. All she had left to do was shower and dress.

Jake entered the bedroom just as she emerged from the bathroom. "I saw the table. You've done a wonderful job. Thanks."

"I wouldn't want Randolph to have room to complain."

He grinned. "That won't stop him. But I appreciate it, even if he doesn't."

"Have Dusty and the boys left?" she asked.

"Just now. They're thrilled at the idea of camping overnight with real cowboys. Chick was so excited, I thought the words would bust right out of him."

"He's going to talk soon, I know he will." Every day the knot of tension and grief that gripped his small body eased a little more. She literally lived for the day when the dam holding back his words finally burst wide open. "Everyone's been so good to him—you and Dusty and the other wranglers. He feels comfortable with all of you. More importantly, he feels safe."

"I'm glad. He's a good kid who's had a rotten break." He took a deep breath, as though gathering strength, and approached. "Listen, I need to talk to you," he said, coming up behind and slipping the towel from her head.

Here it comes, she thought. *Now he'll tell me the truth about this dinner*. "Is there a problem?"

"No problem. But I think you should know... Judge Graydon may ask you some questions."

"What sort of questions?"

"About our marriage." He combed his fingers through her damp hair, caressing her nape. "He's a nosy old man, so just humor him, okay?"

"But you want me to answer his questions?"

"Yes. I'll cut him off if he goes too far."

She turned around, about to reveal what Peter had told her. Then she looked into Jake's eyes, the words dying on her lips unborn. Fierce pride and determination glittered within his golden gaze and in that instant she discovered the answers to all her earlier questions. He hadn't told her the truth about the dinner because he was protecting her, she realized with a sense of wonder, trying to shield her from potential hurt—just as he had when Randolph had accosted her at Belle's, just as he had with the snake. He hoped to pull off tonight without her ever having realized the true purpose of the evening.

Her knight was geared for battle.

"Oh, Jake," she whispered. "Have I ever thanked you for coming into my life?"

He shut his eyes, the muscles knotting in his jaw. "Every day, elf."

She slid her arms around his neck. "It can't possibly be often enough." More than anything she wanted to whisper three tiny words. Three precious, life-altering words. *I love you.* But though it would give her intense joy to speak them, it would cause him intense pain and conflict. And she wouldn't make his life more difficult, not after all he'd done for her and the boys. Unable to resist, she gave him a soft, gentle kiss.

He groaned, his arms tightening around her. "We don't have time for this, do we?"

"Not really. Not if we want to greet our guests when they arrive."

"We could always leave the front door open and put out a make-yourself-at-home sign. If we're long enough, the judge won't even have to ask—" He shut his eyes, his mouth forming a thin, taut line.

"What we've been up to?" she finished lightly.

He released his breath in a gusty sigh. "Yeah."

"How could they doubt it?" she teased. "What woman could possibly resist a man like you?"

His laugh rumbled close to her ear. "You're pretty damned irresistible yourself. Put some clothes on, wife, while I take a shower. Otherwise, I'll say to hell with our guests and take you to bed for the next twenty-four hours.''

''Tempting, Mr. Hondo. Very tempting.''

He kissed her, an intense, passionate kiss that told her more clearly than words how much he wanted her. It gave her hope.

Or was it false hope?

CHAPTER EIGHT

"YOU MUST HAVE BEEN in quite a state when you saw that diamondback," Judge Graydon said, shaking his head in amazement.

"About the same state I was in when Buster tried to ride Mad Dog," Jake retorted dryly. "I think it's called sheer unadulterated terror."

The judge stirred his coffee, his gaze shrewd beneath heavy gray brows. "Having a family is quite a responsibility."

"So I've discovered."

"But worth it?"

Jake glanced at Wynne, the words torn from him. "Yes, it's worth it."

"Oh, please," Randolph muttered in disgust. "What else is he going to say? He'll do whatever it takes to inherit this place. Even lie."

Wynne's coffee cup clattered onto the saucer. "He doesn't lie," she informed him fiercely. "Nor do I. And just so you know, Jake and I did sleep together on our wedding night." She hesitated, then grudgingly conceded, "Actually it was the next morning. But the point is, we're a duly consummated couple. There. Now that we have that out of the way, how about cake?"

"Who told her?" Jake shot to his feet, his scorching gaze pinpointing each dinner guest in turn, before keying in on Peter. "You. This is your doing, isn't it?"

"I—I came by earlier, sure," the lawyer confessed. "But just to make certain everything was set for tonight."

"You son of a—"

"Wait a minute," Peter protested. "Why are you so upset? Didn't *you* tell her what to expect tonight?"

"No, I didn't," Jake snapped.

"But, you said you would."

"I lied!"

"See, he does lie," Randolph said, adding his two-cents' worth.

"Why the hell didn't you explain it to her?" Peter questioned in exasperation. "What did you expect to have happen tonight?"

Jake folded his arms across his chest. "I expected a few subtle questions from the judge. Subtle enough that she wouldn't catch on to the real reason behind his queries."

Judge Graydon frowned in concern. "Why would you keep such a thing from her, Jake?"

He remained silent a long moment, then reluctantly admitted, "I'd hoped to spare her feelings."

"He wanted to protect me," Wynne explained, giving her husband a dazzling smile. "He's just being his usual noble self."

Randolph leapt to his feet, leveling a finger at Jake. "That man hasn't got a noble bone in his body. Nor does he care about anybody's tender feelings. I'll tell you why he kept quiet about that clause... He knew she'd leave him. Any normal woman would, rather than be forced to discuss such intimate details in public."

"Leave him?" Wynne shoved back her chair, her eyes flashing like gemstones. "You think I'm embarrassed or humiliated to admit I'm Jake's wife in the truest sense of the word? I'm proud of it. I'd announce it to the entire world, if he asked me."

"He's using you," Randolph retorted, resentment gathering in his voice. "You must be blind not to see it."

"If that's what you believe, you can't know Jake very well," she stated with absolute conviction.

"I've known him for years. Unfortunately." He glared at her in frustration. "You seem to have the mistaken impression that he's some sort of domesticated lap cat. Well, you're wrong. The man is a vicious predator who wandered over from the wrong side of the tracks. And the minute you turn your back on him, he's going to rip you to shreds."

Jake returned to his seat, a lazy smile creeping across his face. "Please, Chesterfield. Don't bother to pull your punches." He tipped the chair back onto two legs. "You've been dying to tell me what you really think for years now. Well, here's your chance."

"You're right. I have wanted to tell you what I think." Randolph's jaw clenched, his entire body tensing in anticipation. "And with the judge as a witness, you wouldn't dare attack me for speaking the truth."

"Your version of the truth." Jake corrected him mildly.

"Mine and everyone else's in this town." Randolph planted his palms on the tabletop. "You're a no-good louse, Hondo, with an eye on the main chance, just like your mother. The only difference between you two is she didn't have your luck. If the old man hadn't been so desperate for a grandson, he'd never have taken you in."

Jake shrugged. "Old news, Chesterfield. My grandfather made that very clear when he came for me. If he'd had any legitimate grandchildren, I'd have been left in the gutter where he found me. So what? I never wanted to go with him in the first place. If the courts hadn't enforced his request, I'd have stayed put. At least I knew where I stood on the streets."

"But you did come back with him. And then you rode into town intent on getting even with anyone who'd known your mother—"

The front legs of Jake's chair crashed to the wooden floor. "I didn't ride in, I was driven. Or should I say hog-tied and dragged, fighting every damned inch of the way? It'd be more accurate."

"You wanted to get even because we all stood by while Chesterfield threw your mother off his land."

Jake laughed, the sound more chilling than a bitter arctic wind. "He didn't throw her off. Hell, he didn't have to. All it took was a few coins chucked into the dirt and she left of her own accord, grateful for that much."

"Nonetheless, you came back to get even because no one lifted a finger to help her. You blackened every eye that looked at you sideways and forced yourself on every woman who wandered within reach."

Evie stood and crossed to her husband's side. "Randolph, stop. You don't know what you're saying."

"I know exactly what I'm saying. And it's time the sweet, faithful Mrs. Hondo knew, too." He shot Wynne a mocking look. "How do you like the truth so far?"

"Which truth? That Jake's illegitimate?" She shrugged. "He told me. Since that's not his fault, I can hardly hold him responsible ... though apparently you do."

"I hold him responsible for his actions since coming to town. Or doesn't it bother you that he speaks with his fists and can't be trusted around any decent woman?"

"If you think I'm shocked that Jake has been in a few brawls, you're sadly mistaken. Of course he gets into fights. All you have to do is look at the man to know that you provoke him at your own risk." Wynne smiled proudly. "He's a natural-born warrior. That's one of the reasons I married him."

"You can't be serious!"

"I'm quite serious. And as far as women are concerned ... I assure you, he would never force himself on anyone. He wouldn't have to."

A harsh laugh burst from Randolph. "I know for a fact that he's done just that."

"Please, don't say more," Evie urged her husband. "It won't change anything."

Wynne refused to back down. Randolph was maligning *her* husband, and that was one challenge she couldn't allow to pass uncontested. Slowly rising to her feet, she flung her linen napkin onto the table as though it were a gauntlet. "Women may claim they were forced," she informed him in clear, precise tones. "But only because they didn't have the nerve to admit the truth."

"And what truth is that?"

"That they allowed themselves to be seduced by the town's black sheep."

She'd clearly struck a chord. Hot color washed into Randolph's face. "That's a lie!"

Jake didn't say a word, simply raised his wineglass in salute, the tender expression in his eyes tearing at her heart. It was all the encouragement she needed.

"It's not a lie, but a shameful truth," she retorted. "How many women, I wonder, who wouldn't give my husband the time of day in public, slipped eagerly into his bed in the dead of night? Five, ten . . ." She glanced at Jake and lifted an eyebrow. "More?"

"It was before I knew you, elf," he said without apology. "I hope you're not offended."

"I'm not the least offended. It was their loss, not mine. They only knew half the man. I intend to know the whole."

"When's the next Cinderella Ball?" Peter demanded. "I want a wife like her."

"She's lying I tell you!" The words burst from Randolph, laden with helpless fury. "She's so hot for Hondo she'll make up any story to protect him." He scowled at her. "You may have been an easy tumble for him, but my wife never was!"

"*Randolph*!" Evie cried.

Wynne didn't waste her breath trying to stop the fight brewing. She could tell Jake was blind to everything but the overwhelming urge to get at his cousin. Instead, she darted around the table, throwing herself at Jake to physically restrain him. His muscles bunched beneath her hands and he caught her shoulders as though he intended to force her from his path. But it was Evie's plea that ultimately checked his threatening move toward Randolph.

"Jake, I beg you. Don't touch him," she whispered. "He doesn't know what he's saying."

The breath shuddered through his body as he fought to bring his anger under control. "Get out of my house, Chesterfield. Quick," Jake warned in a low, grating voice. "And don't come near me again for a long, long time. Otherwise you'll pay a hard price for that crack."

Randolph didn't need any further encouragement. Wrapping an arm around Evie, he fled the room.

"Make sure he leaves without causing any more trouble," Jake said to Peter. "I'll talk to you in the morning."

"No problem. Time I was getting home, anyway."

Jake turned on Judge Graydon next. "Have you heard what you came for?" he demanded. "Because as far as I'm concerned, you can all go to hell. I'm not answering any more questions, and neither is my wife."

"Easy, son," the judge said, holding up his hands. "You and Wynne have satisfied the terms of the will. The property is legally yours." His gray brows pulled together. "I hope for your sake, however, that Randolph is wrong."

"Wrong about what?"

He nodded toward Wynne. "This wife of yours is good for you, Jake. You won't find better. It's none of my business, but I sincerely hope that this marriage is more than just a sham."

The muscles in Jake's jaw tightened. "You're right. It's none of your business. My grandfather had no call putting such an unreasonable condition in his will. You can safely assume that any loopholes I find are fair game."

"He put that marital clause in there for your sake, my boy."

"Bull! He did it to ensure the continuation of his line. He was obsessed with siring a dynasty."

"Knowing Weston, that probably played a part in his decision," Graydon conceded. "But that wasn't the real purpose. There was another, more important reason."

Jake's expression turned derisive. "Yeah, right. Why don't you tell me what his 'real' reason was? It ought to be good for a laugh, if nothing else."

Graydon sighed. "He wanted to give you the one thing you've never had."

That gave him pause. "And what was that?"

"Sorry, Jake. I'm not going to make it easy for you." The judge glanced at Wynne. "Besides, if you don't figure out the answer soon, then Weston failed and it won't matter anyway."

"He wanted to give me a wife?" Jake demanded in frustration. It didn't make sense. "Legitimate children? I could have taken care of that myself. It wouldn't have been difficult to arrange."

"Oh, Jake," Wynne whispered. "You don't just buy those things."

"No?" He gave a cynical laugh. "My grandfather spent a lifetime demonstrating just the opposite. He took great pleasure in proving you can buy anyone and everything."

"No, not everything. And that's what your grand-father finally did learn," she responded quietly. Arguing with him would be fruitless, she realized then. Judging by the set of his jaw, she didn't have a hope of altering his stance on the subject. She turned to the judge and offered her hand. "Thank you for coming. I apologize that the evening got a little heated."

"Only to be expected." He gathered her hand in his. "It's been a real pleasure meeting you, my dear. I hope to see a lot more of you in future."

"Time will tell," she replied obliquely.

With that, the judge left. Jake shut the door behind him with pointed finality. "Quite some party you throw, Mrs. Hondo."

"It was...interesting," she agreed. "I suspect it will be the topic of discussion for a long time to come."

"Around here that kind of discussion is called gossip. And I'm afraid you're right. If we weren't the talk of the town before, we will be now." He thrust a hand through his hair and glanced at her speculatively. "Care for a drink? I don't know about you, but I could sure use one."

"Sounds perfect."

He led the way into a very masculine library. Steel-gray carpet covered the floor. At one end of the room was a sturdy rolltop desk and a massive captain's chair, flanked on three sides by built-in bookcases. Opposite the desk, a huge stone fireplace took up the whole of one wall.

"Do you use that often?" she asked, nodding toward the hearth.

"From Christmas on, Grandfather always kept it lit." He handed her a snifter of brandy and swept aside the wire mesh screen protecting the grate. "Care for a fire tonight?" he asked, poking at the wood staked inside.

"It hasn't gotten very cold out, yet, but I'm in the mood for one anyway."

"Sounds wonderful." Crossing to the switch by the door, she flipped off the overhead light so the small blaze he'd started provided the sole illumination. "Better?"

"Yeah, much." He settled on the carpet in front of the hearth and took a healthy swallow of brandy. "Jeez, I'm glad that damn dinner is over."

"So am I," she said, joining him. "I'm also glad the boys weren't here. I shudder to think what they'd have done to Randolph if they had been."

"No worse than what I'd have done if he'd said one more word to you."

A topic best avoided, she decided. "It's going to seem strange tonight...having the boys gone, I mean."

"You usually tuck them in at bedtime, don't you?"

She nodded, confessing, "I like to sit and watch them sleep."

"Do they remind you of your sister? What was her name? Tracy?"

"Yes." Wynne bowed her head. "I feel closer to both her and Rob when I'm with the boys. I can..." She shrugged. "I can feel them nearby."

"They must have thought a lot of you to leave their kids in your care."

"They knew I loved Buster and Chick," she answered simply. "That I'd do anything for them."

"Even marry me."

Her smile held a whimsical charm. "That was the easiest decision I ever made. I realized the minute we met that you were the perfect man."

"Because I could slay dragons." Shadows concealed his expression, but his voice held a caustic edge.

"Not just that. You were the perfect man because I—" *Because I took one look and saw you more clearly than you see yourself. Because the moment I looked into your fierce golden eyes, I fell impossibly, irrevocably in love.* But she couldn't tell him that, he wasn't ready to hear it. So she offered the only response he'd find palatable. "I married you because we needed each other. We still do."

"For a little longer." His words held a grim warning.

"Jake..."

He released his breath in a gusty sigh. "Let me guess... What part of the evening do you want to hash out? The part about my grandfather? My parents? My untempered pillaging of the women in town?"

"I think we settled the issue of your pillaging, untempered or otherwise," she replied with a quick grin.

"Thanks to your impassioned defense."

"Don't sound so surprised. I know what sort of man you are, even if Randolph doesn't. I also know that it's ridiculous to believe you'd resort to force when you could seduce any woman in town with a single look."

His laughter sounded rusty. "It might take a little more effort than just a look."

"Maybe." She cast him a sidelong glance. "But one lesson on how to drive your truck would have overcome any lingering hesitation on their part."

He shook his head, lounging on his elbow. "No way, sweetpea. You're the only woman I've ever taught to drive a stick shift." His eyes darkened. "The only woman I'd care to teach, for that matter."

"I'm glad to hear it," she admitted with a shy smile. She scooted closer to him, sliding her hand across his thigh. Flames leapt behind the screen, the firelight branding her pale hair with crimson streaks and flickering across the pure planes of her face. "Tell me the rest, Jake," she urged. "Tell me quickly so it's off your chest and we don't have to ever refer to it again."

"You want to hear all the gory details of my life?"

"Not really. But I suspect you need to tell them to me—for your own well-being."

He instantly withdrew, the mental barriers slamming into place. "Why would you think that?" he asked coldly.

"It's all right, Jake. I won't run screaming in terror once I know your darkest secrets. I won't turn from you in disgust or treat you with pity. And I certainly won't sneak into your bed in the middle of the night, then pretend we're strangers come daybreak." She paused. "That is why you haven't told me, isn't it? Because you weren't certain how I'd react."

He sat up abruptly. "Damn you," he whispered.

"I know," she sympathized. "You've worked so hard to build up your defenses, secured every wall, made sure your fortress is totally invulnerable. Now you have this irritating wife, banging on the castle door and you have to open up and let her in."

"I *have* to?"

She gave him an impish grin. "Just this once. After that, you can sling her out into the cold and simply ignore her."

"You're a hard woman to ignore," he retorted.

"So you've said. Annoying, pesky, tenacious."

The gold of his eyes rivaled the hot glow of the fire. "And loyal as hell. Okay, wife. You've heard most of the sordid details. There's not much left to the story." He stood and tossed another log onto the iron grate. "My parents met, fell in lust and had a summer of careless pleasure. Careless because they accidentally conceived me. When my mother found out she was pregnant, she approached my father. Sorry, he said, he'd just gotten engaged to someone else—a socially acceptable someone else—and he'd appreciate it if she'd disappear. To ensure it, my grandfather made it worth her while."

"He paid her."

"And thus helped cement her choice of careers."

"Oh, Jake," Wynne murmured.

"No pity, remember?" he bit out. "When I turned sixteen she died and I ended up on the streets. By that time, my father had also met an untimely end. His wife had never been able to bear him any children and my grandfather was desperate. Remembering the pregnant girl he'd bought off all those years ago, he came looking for me."

"And returned to Chesterfield with a furious, resentful teenager." It wasn't a question.

"I sure as hell wasn't the grandson he'd dreamt of having. I despised him for his hypocrisy and made no bones about it. In exchange for my hatred, he gave me all he possessed. Food, clothes, a roof over my head... Everything money could buy, he provided without hesitation. The one thing he asked in exchange I refused to give him."

It only took a moment's thought to figure out what Jake had withheld. "Your name."

He nodded. "For years Grandfather begged me to change it to Chesterfield. But I refused."

She eyed him shrewdly. "It was the only way you could keep your own identity, to keep that last piece of yourself intact."

He shrugged. "I was Jake Hondo and calling me Chesterfield wouldn't change the circumstances surrounding my birth."

"But you grew to love him, didn't you, despite what he'd done to your mother?"

He ran a hand across his nape. "Yeah," he admitted. "I did. He was a proud, lonely man who'd made a lot of mistakes in his life. And not once did he ever try to justify those mistakes or place the blame elsewhere. He just stood up and said, 'I'm the one.' I respected him for that, if nothing else.''

"But you didn't stay with him, did you?"

He sighed. "I presume you're asking about Lost Trail."

"Yes."

"From the minute I arrived in Chesterfield, I started working and saving so I could buy my own place."

She nodded in perfect understanding. "That independent streak of yours—never depend on anyone or anything."

"Something like that," he agreed. "I got lucky. When I was in my mid-twenties, the neighboring ranch came available and I bought it. It was pitifully small compared to what my grandfather owned, but little by little I acquired the surrounding land until I had a respectable-sized spread."

"But Dusty said you didn't stay there, that you moved back in with your grandfather."

"Not long after I made the purchase, the doctors discovered he had cancer." He stared at the fire, his face an expressionless mask. "What else could I do?"

"*You* couldn't have done anything else," she informed him. "Another person might have been more callous."

"I'm callous enough. And just so you know how callous..." He gave her a cool, direct look. "I could have brought you here after the wedding. Instead I chose to take you and the boys to Lost Trail. Care to know why?" He didn't wait for her to answer, just gave her the hard, cold facts. "I didn't want you to get your hopes up about staying, didn't want you to get too comfortable living with me. That way there wouldn't be any regrets when the time came to leave."

Amusement brightened her eyes. "Do you think when I leave I'll miss the ranch more than the man?" She'd set him back on his heels with that one, she realized, stifling the urge to laugh.

"Most women would," he muttered, then held up his hands. "I know, I know. You're not most women. Maybe I should write that down so I don't forget. You have a pen handy?"

"Don't worry, I'll keep reminding you."

"I don't doubt it." He lifted an eyebrow. "Are we done?"

"Just one or two more questions," she assured. "Tell me about Randolph."

Jake grimaced. "Randolph's a couple years older. Until I appeared on the scene, he considered himself the heir apparent, despite his distant connection. It was a nasty shock to discover his error. From the minute I arrived, it became his goal to make my life a misery."

"And Evie?"

He shook his head. "Sorry, elf. That's a private matter."

"No problem. I have a pretty good idea about what happened there."

"Why doesn't that surprise me?" he muttered.

He took a quick swallow of brandy, as though screwing up his courage—which was utterly ridiculous. Jake was the bravest man she knew. "What is it?" she asked gently.

His breath escaped in a harsh laugh. "You don't miss much do you?"

"I try not to," she confessed with a shrug. "Is there something else you want to tell me?"

"Not tell you exactly. I want to thank you."

Her brows winged upward. "For what?"

"For tonight." He leaned closer and cupped her face, his thumb tracing the generous curve of her mouth. "And I wanted to apologize. I should have told you the

true reason for tonight's gathering. I didn't because...
Because..."

She leaned into his touch. "Because you wanted to
protect me from embarrassment."

He closed his eyes, a muscle jerking in his cheek. "No,
dammit. That's not the reason. It's the excuse I used,
but it isn't the truth. I was afraid to tell you about that
clause in my grandfather's will. I was afraid of what
you'd do."

She gazed at him in bewilderment. "I don't understand. You're not afraid of anything."

"I didn't think so." He looked at her then, holding
her with a fathomless golden gaze. "Until I met you.
You scare the living hell out of me, sweetpea."

The words hung between them—simple, brutally frank
and utterly devastating. "You're afraid of *me*?" she
whispered, shocked. "*Why*?"

He didn't want to answer, didn't want to reveal another
chink in his armor. But she deserved his honesty, if
nothing else. "You're the first person ever to believe in
me. To offer unconditional trust. You see people so
clearly. And yet when you look at me, you see someone
I don't know." His mouth twisted in a self-deprecating
smile. "Don't you understand? That image, that man
you've created for yourself isn't real. And the one who
does exist can only hurt you."

"Then one of us is wrong. And just in case you were
wondering..." Her eyes gathered up the firelight, reflecting its fierce heat and energy. "It's not me."

It seemed an eternity before he could respond. "What
am I going to do with you?" he asked roughly.

The answer trembled on her lips, but she caught the
words just in time, altering them ever so slightly. "Make
love to me."

His laughter came easier now. "That shouldn't be too
difficult. I can't keep my hands off you."

"I don't remember asking you to."

His hand slipped from her cheek to curve around her neck. "Come here." He exerted the slightest pressure, tumbling her into his arms.

Their mouths collided and their limbs entwined, an overwhelming urgency setting the mating dance into motion. Though he'd taught her the steps well, she'd come into her own over the past weeks, bringing a unique style and grace to the ritual. Completely unselfconscious, she rose to her knees and shed her clothing. She didn't tantalize, didn't tease, nor did she display any uncertainty in this moment of utter vulnerability. She simply gifted him with her body, offering herself, heart and soul, without hesitation or reserve. It had always been this way with her.

And it never failed to humble him.

Finally the last of her clothes were removed and she knelt, poised before him. She was made for firelight, he determined in that moment. The glow from the leaping flames licked at the alabaster hillocks of her breasts before melting into the shadowy delta at the juncture of her thighs. He reached for her and froze.

The deep bronze of his hand stood out like a stark blemish against the pale perfection of her skin, the contrast between them as startling as it was unwelcome.

How could she not have noticed? he wondered in despair. She was heavenly light battling hellish darkness, the rich, warm earth fighting the intrusion of stone and brick and cement. She offered the eternal hope of spring during the deepest despair of winter. She was all he could ever want, offering possibilities that could never be his.

"Don't," she whispered. He jerked his hand back as though burned and she laughed gently, the sound a welcome balm. "I didn't mean not to touch me. I meant—don't think. Don't analyze. Don't question it." She took the initiative, gathering him into her arms.

"Just for tonight, won't you lock your demons outside? They're not going anywhere, are they?"

"No," he conceded, warning, "they'll still be waiting come morning."

"Then we'll worry about them tomorrow."

She was right. This moment offered a respite between battles, and he'd be a fool not to take advantage of it. With infinite tenderness he rolled them onto the carpet, anointing her with mouth and tongue and teeth. He felt the first flush of desire wash across her skin like a storm-driven tide, and he cupped her breast, the frantic pounding of her heart filling his palm. She twisted beneath him, lifting her hips to mesh with his, moving with all the sinuous grace of a sun-warmed feline.

He tried to go slow, but desire became a rapacious hunger, a demand that turned his kisses hard and urgent and made each caress more aggressive than the last. He reveled in the delicious mix of passionate heat and fluid softness, sinking into her warmth, then driving into it, compelled by a force too powerful to resist. He heard her frantic sobs, responded to the incoherent pleas, wanting more than life itself to give her the release she so desperately sought. He angled her hips upward, melding his mouth with hers. Instantly her muscles tensed in reaction and she exploded in his arms. It was all he needed. With a harsh cry, he drove home, following her over the edge. In that instant, their eyes met.

And what he saw there knifed deep into his soul.

For in those misty green depths he saw love. A permanent love—pure and faithful and absolute. He knew then that she'd given a forever-after love to a temporary husband.

And with that terrible knowledge, the demons came storming back.

CHAPTER NINE

JAKE WOKE several hours later, struggling to get his bearings in the pitch-black room. His muscles protested the amount of time he'd spent sleeping on the floor and yet he hesitated to disturb Wynne. She lay curled on her side, tucked tightly into the protective curve of his body. The fire had died long ago and a new moon, skulking in the shadow of the earth, ducked between bits of starlight as it traversed the nighttime sky. Gingerly he eased the cramp plaguing his leg.

With a gusty sigh, Wynne rolled over to face him. "What time is it?" she murmured.

"Time for bed, wife. Do you want your own room, or would you rather sleep with me?"

She yawned. "I don't know why you even bother to ask."

"I'm asking because we're in a new place. And after the dinner party..."

"New or otherwise, my place is with you," she told him firmly and snuggled deeper into his arms.

Something in her words revived the memory of their earlier lovemaking. He remembered the expression in her eyes—the one that spoke of miracles and storybook endings and eternities. He didn't doubt that look had returned. It was in her voice, in her touch, in her soft, eager kisses.

The urge to distance himself became overwhelming. "Your place may be with me for now," he warned harshly, "but sleeping in my bed won't seduce me into

151

keeping you any longer than necessary. What does that figure out to—a few days, a week, a month?''

His coldheartedness went unnoticed. "It doesn't matter how many days we have," she countered. "We also have an equal number of nights. And I want each one to be wonderful—a beautiful memory you can recall when I'm long gone and half-forgotten.''

Her unstinting generosity was more crippling than any protest or tears or recriminations. He stood, sweeping her into his arms, and strode purposefully from the room. "Let's find a bed. We may only have here and now, but we can turn it into one hell of a memory for later.''

"When memories are all we have left?" she asked wistfully.

But he didn't answer, was incapable of answering. For even if he found the right words, he'd never have gotten them past the tight knot blocking his throat.

The boys returned late the next day, exhausted and excited and bursting to tell Wynne and Jake all about their adventures.

"And then this big, old bull came right at Dusty," Buster told them, his feet spread wide, his Stetson tipped back on his head in perfect imitation of Jake's stance. "I thought he was a goner for sure.''

Chick tugged on his brother's elbow, whispering rapidly. Buster shook him off. "But Dusty didn't budge one bit. All's he did was spit. It was so cool.''

"You weren't in any danger, were you?" Wynne questioned in alarm.

"Naw. They made us stay clear of all the good stuff.''

Chick sidled closer to his brother, whispering more urgently.

"Not now," Buster replied in annoyance. "I'm not done with my story, yet. So then Dusty whipped out his lasso and roped that critter slick as you please. See you gotta get one rope around the cow and the other around this thing on the saddle.''

"Saddlehorn." Jake tossed out the word.

"Yeah. Saddlehorn. That way the horse does the work and not the cowboy. But you have to wrap the rope around so's you don't lose no fingers. Dusty called it dal— Dal-something."

"Dallying."

Buster grinned at Jake. "Yeah, dallying. Will you teach me how to do it? Huh, Dad? Will you?" His words stumbled to a halt as he realized what he'd said and he turned white as a sheet. Shooting a stricken look in Wynne's direction, he turned and ran from the room.

Jake swore beneath his breath. "I'll talk to him," he said to Wynne.

She caught his arm. "Please, let me."

He gave a terse nod, and, gathering Chick close, she followed at a discreet distance. She could hear Buster's frantic sobs coming from his room and entered, crossing to sit on the bed next to him. Chick glued himself to her other side. Gently she ruffled her nephew's sun-streaked hair. "Are you all right?"

"I didn't mean to call him that," Buster managed to say through his tears. "I know he's not my dad. You told us we're just staying with him for a little while. He's a temp... Temp—"

"Temporary," Wynne supplied regretfully.

"Yeah, a temporary husband. I remember you telling us all that. About how marrying Jake is like a summer job except it's during the winter. Only..." Tears threatened again. "Only I wish we didn't never have to leave."

"I know." Those two simple words spoke volumes.

"Why can't we stay?" He lifted his head to look at her. "I like it here. Chick does, too."

Chick nodded, his pleading gaze matching Buster's.

"I'm sorry, but that's not fair to Jake." She swallowed, struggling for composure. "You see, I promised that we'd only stay for a little while. I can't go back on my word. It wouldn't be right."

"Can't you ask him to change his mind? If he says yes, that wouldn't be going back on your word." He threw himself into Wynne's arms. "Please let us stay. We'll be good. And we won't make no more trouble. I promise."

Hearing the desperation in her nephew's voice, she closed her eyes. If she didn't see his pain, perhaps she wouldn't be tempted to give in to it. Because refusing Buster's request was the hardest thing she'd ever done in her life, especially when she wanted it as badly as did he. "I'm sorry," she whispered, fighting back tears of her own. "Please try to understand. I can't. When the time comes, we'll have to leave."

With a silent groan, Jake leaned against the wall, his hands balled in fists, his teeth clenched. This wasn't what he'd planned. This wasn't what he wanted. He'd never intended to inflict such hurt. Dammit to hell! Why did he destroy everything he touched? Just once in his life he'd like to be the fantasy man Wynne saw, rather than the man fate had dictated. Just this once he wished... He straightened, his spine rigid, his mouth a taut line. Who was he kidding? Wishes weren't for men like him.

They never had been. They never could be.

Jake examined another receipt and checked the total, a distant sound breaking his concentration. He looked up briefly, before returning his attention to the invoices spread across his desk. Hours had passed since that incident in the hallway and he'd closeted himself in the library, focusing on a backlog of paperwork. It was a blessing not to think, not to feel, just to go through the daily grind like some computerized automaton.

The sound came again, and he frowned, tossing his pencil onto the desk. Now what? He crossed to the door and opened it, the sound assailing his ears shocking him so badly, that for an instant he froze. Another heart-breaking sob was all it took to send him tearing down the hallway. He careened off the wall and skidded into the kitchen. Wynne sat crouched in the middle of the floor, her face buried in her hands, quietly crying. Slowly he sank to his knees next to her, feeling as though he'd been sucker-punched. Except for that single, gut-wrenching tear she'd shed on their wedding night, he'd never seen Wynne cry before. Not like this. Not like her heart was breaking.

"What's wrong?" he demanded, afraid to touch her, searching frantically for an injury.

With a hiccupped sob, she thrust out her hand and shook it beneath his nose.

He took her fingers gingerly in his. No cuts or abrasions, thank heavens. No swelling. No joints out of place. His brows drew together. "Talk to me, sweetpea. Where are you hurt?"

"I—I'm not hurt!" she answered in tragic tones.

"Then what the hell—heck are you crying for?" he demanded, relief bringing an exasperated tone to his voice.

She lifted her head, her huge green eyes overflowing. She shook her hand at him again. "I l-lost it! It went down the dr-drain."

He stared at her hand—her *left* hand and understanding dawned. "Your wedding ring. Your wedding ring washed down the drain?" Fresh tears broke loose and, taking them as confirmation, he gathered her into his arms. "It's all right. Don't cry. We'll get you another one."

It was the wrong thing to say. Her crying intensified. "I d-don't want another one! I want our r-ring. Th-the one you gave me when we got married."

Before he could reply, Buster and Chick slid to a halt in the doorway, followed closely by Dusty. "Told you she was crying," Buster said.

"What happened to her?" the foreman demanded. "What's wrong with the girl?"

"Her wedding ring went down the drain," Jake explained tersely. "Go get a wrench, will you?"

"We'll have better luck with a shovel," Dusty replied with a snort. "Most likely we'll have to dig up the whole septic system to find the dang thing."

Wynne shuddered in his arms and Jake glared at his foreman. "If I'd wanted your opinion on the matter, I'd have beat it out of you. Just get the damn-dang shovel, will you?"

"I'm a-goin', I'm a-goin'. No need to git yer britches in a bunch." Dusty shot the boys a meaningful glance. "The two of you best be careful. Bad luck comes in threes, ya know." And with that telling comment, he took off.

Unfortunately he was soon proved right. Not an hour later, Jake broke his hand tearing up the plumbing.

And the day after that Mrs. Marsh arrived.

"Go to the barn and get Jake," Wynne ordered the boys, as she watched their aunt step from her rental car. "Then play upstairs until I call you. Jake and I would like to speak with her in private."

"What's she here for? What does she want?" Buster questioned apprehensively.

"I'm sure she wants to meet Jake and see how you two are doing."

"Is she going to take us away?"

Wynne gave the boys a quick hug. "Of course not. Everything will be fine. She's just here for a little visit."

Chick whispered in Buster's ear and, obliging his brother, he asked, "Do we have to go to that school of hers? The one that won't let us be together?"

"Not a chance. Now hurry and get Jake."

It seemed an eternity before he finally emerged from the barn. Joining her in the kitchen, he washed up while she brewed tea. "That woman parked in the parlor is your dragon?" he questioned in amusement. "You sure her name is Marsh and not Marshmallow?"

"You'll see," Wynne predicted ominously. "Don't let all those smiles and dimples fool you. She's as tough as old shoe leather."

"Why do you call her Mrs. Marsh? Doesn't she have a first name?"

"It's Kitty, but not even the boys are allowed to use it. I have permission to address her as Mrs. Marsh or ma'am." She gritted her teeth. "Needless to say, I refuse to call her ma'am."

"And I thought taking care of your dragon-lady was going to be tough." Jake picked up the laden tray awkwardly and grinned. "Lead the way, fair maiden. I have a kitty to slew. Or is it slay?"

"Just watch your back," she retorted. "Or you'll find out which it is."

It took a whole thirty seconds for him to discover the truth behind Wynne's warning.

Mrs. Marsh, a fragile-looking woman in her early forties, took a dainty sip of tea, fixed guileless powder-blue eyes on Jake and flashed her dimples. "I do hate wasting precious time on preliminaries," she announced. "Why don't we get right down to business?"

Jake lifted an eyebrow. "I didn't realize you and I had any business."

"We didn't." She stared pointedly at Wynne. "Until very recently."

He shrugged. "So talk. I'm listening."

"You have a very fine ranch here." She wrinkled her tiny nose as though smelling something unpleasant. "Assuming you like ranches."

"I gather you don't." Not that there was much doubt about her opinion.

"No," she confirmed. "But my sources say this is one of the better ones, which must be why you went to such lengths to keep it. I refer, of course, to your marriage." She returned her teacup to its saucer and lifted a finely arched eyebrow. "A condition of your grandfather's will or some such thing?"

The dragon-lady had been busy making inquiries. Who had she spoken to? Or perhaps the better question was... who *hadn't* she spoken to? "Yeah, it was a condition of his will. So?"

"So... Now that you have legal control of your inheritance, you don't need a wife anymore."

His eyes narrowed. "According to you."

"And according to most everyone in town. Wynne and the boys are excess baggage and it's only a matter of time before you toss them out the door."

"Did you hear that, elf?" Ignoring proper decorum, he propped a booted foot on the coffee table. "Folks around here think I'll be putting you out with the garbage."

Wynne muttered something uncomplimentary and he couldn't help but wonder if it was aimed at the Marsh woman—or at him.

"Please, Mr. Hondo. Let's be frank." Kitty Marsh leaned back in her chair and crossed her legs. "Now that your inheritance is secure, you don't need the pretence of a family anymore. Sooner or later, you're going to

get rid of them. I'm willing to make it worth your while
to make it sooner."

"How much?" he asked out of curiosity. Wynne
gasped in disbelief, but he ignored her, keeping his gaze
trained on the viper seated across from him. He'd learned
long ago never to take his eyes off a snake poised to
strike and he didn't intend to start now.

The Marsh woman smiled in triumph. "How much
would you like?"

"I can't say," he confessed, running a hand across his
jaw. "To be honest, I have just about all the money I
could ever hope to spend."

"Then perhaps I can offer something else." Her smile
turned provocative. "I'm open to suggestions."

"Don't bother trying to seduce him," Wynne snapped.
"He's not interested in married women."

"Well... Only one," Jake said with a lazy grin.

"Then we'll stick to material assets," Mrs. Marsh retorted, her smile fading. "What will you take in exchange for the children?"

"Why do you want them?" he countered.

She shrugged. "Why does a person want diamonds
or furs or a new car? It's an uncontrollable urge. Maternal instinct or something."

Maternal instinct in a pig's eye. He'd never met a
woman less cut out for motherhood than this one.
"Forget it," he stated flatly, tiring of her game.

"I didn't answer that right, did I?" she asked in
amusement. "Okay, how about this...?" Crocodile tears
welled into her eyes. "They're all that's left of my poor,
dear brother. I have so much to offer them, so much to
give. And since I could never have children of my
own—"

"Oh, *please*!" Wynne cut her off. "You never wanted
children. You said they'd ruin your figure, that they
were messy."

Her tears vanished as quickly as they'd come. "But don't you see? That's what makes it all so perfect. No horrid pregnancy, no smelly, squally babies. And best of all they're housebroken." She turned on Jake. "Now, how much?"

"I'm not for sale and neither are they."

"I don't think you understand." Her voice hardened. "I'm really quite desperate here. I'll do whatever it takes to get my hands on those boys."

"Brad wants them, doesn't he?" Wynne guessed shrewdly.

Fury robbed her face of all beauty. "Yes. After all these years, my dear husband has decided he wants kids and I suspect he's looking around for someone young and nubile enough to provide them. Buster and Chick are my only hope."

Jake laughed. "I'm all broken up over your marital problems, lady. But that doesn't change my mind. The boys stay here."

Her eyes darkened, the blue turning as dull and garish as fake sapphires. "Assuming that's your final word on the matter, we'll move on to threats."

He didn't look worried. "And what would those be?"

"If you don't give me the children, I'll take Wynne to court."

"On what grounds?"

"I think my concern for the safety of the children should do the trick. Since arriving in Texas, they've been forced to stay in a run-down shack when they could have been housed here. They've attempted to ride the most dangerous horse in several counties. And they've come within a breath of being bitten by one of the deadliest snakes in the country." She tilted her head to one side. "Have I overlooked anything?"

Panic appeared in Wynne's eyes. "How did you find out about that?"

Jake didn't need to ask. "Randolph! The son of a
b—"

"Yes, Mr. Hondo?" Mrs. Marsh prompted with a cold
smile. "You were about to say?"

He gritted his teeth. "Never mind."

"I'll be sure to add your vulgarity to my list of con-
cerns—assuming I can find the room. It's a very long
list." She switched her attention to Wynne. "I'm here
to offer you a choice. You can turn the children over to
me now and I'll allow you to continue seeing them. Or
you can force me to endure the cost and annoyance of
a court hearing. In which case I'll make sure you never
see the boys again."

"That's not a choice," Jake snapped. "It's a threat."

"Actually, Mr. Hondo, it's a promise. One I intend
to keep." She gathered up her purse. "I believe that con-
cludes our business. I'll give you some time to discuss
my offer, not that there's anything *to* discuss. When you
reach your decision, I can be contacted in town at the
Bluebonnet Inn. Dreadful name, but pleasant enough
accommodations considering I'm in Texas."

"Don't you want to see your nephews before you
leave?" Jake questioned with heavy irony.

"No need. I'll see them soon enough. I plan to have
them home with me by Thanksgiving." She stood.
"Please don't get up. I can find my own way."

"And do me out of the pleasure of showing you the
door?" Jake snarled as he gained his feet. "I wouldn't
hear of it."

She drew back. "Are you threatening me with physical harm?"

"I don't threaten, either, Mrs. Marsh. Like you, I only
make promises."

Her composure shaken, she backed toward the door.
"Is that how you broke your hand, in a brawl? My list

gets longer by the second. And my concern for my nephews grows along with it.''

Predictably, Wynne leapt to his defense. "If you think he'd ever do anything to harm them, you're sadly mistaken. He's the sweetest, kindest, gentlest man in the world."

A reluctant grin snagged Jake's mouth. "Give it up, elf. Even I have trouble swallowing that one."

"As would anyone who's met him," added Mrs. Marsh. "I look forward to your call." Gathering the shreds of her dignity, she marched from the room. A moment later the front door banged close, signaling her departure.

The boys crept silently up the steps to their room.

"Come on, Chick. I've got a plan," Buster said with grim resolve. "She can't take us away if she can't find us. So we'll just hide until she goes away or finds some other kids to be nice to or something."

Chick whispered a question.

"Yeah, I guess they will be worried." He brightened. "We'll leave them a note. But we won't tell them where we'll be. That way nobody can make us go with Aunt Marsh if she wins the fight."

"What are we going to do?" Wynne asked, struggling to keep the panic from her voice.

"For now, we wait."

"But what about her threats?"

Jake shrugged. "Even if she takes us to court, I doubt she'd win. For one thing, we're still together, despite local gossip."

Wynne frowned. But for how long? Too bad she didn't have the nerve to ask. "What about her other complaints—you know, about Mad Dog and the snake?"

He grimaced. "I admit, the boys have gotten into a scrape or two, but it hasn't hurt them any. And as Mrs. Marsh pointed out, this is Texas. There's not a single kid around these parts who hasn't been bucked off a horse or come toe to fang with a rattler. I'm hoping the judge will see her as a sweet, if unduly apprehensive relative." His expression turned sour. "I assume she can play the sweet and caring aunt when it's in her best interest."

"She's a master at it," Wynne assured grimly. "The dimples alone could convince a card-carrying pessimist that the glass is half full. And if they don't do the trick, she turns on the waterworks."

"So I saw." He shuddered. "Heaven protect me from weepy women."

Wynne glanced at her bare left ring finger and bit her lip.

He caught the direction of her glance. "I'm sorry, sweetheart," he said with a sigh. "I didn't mean you. You had cause to shed a few tears. I just wish I could have found the darned thing."

"It's not your fault," she whispered. "I should have had it sized."

He tugged her into his arms. "Let me replace it. We can go into town and buy one that actually fits. It might even help convince Mrs. Marsh—" He broke off at her expression. "I'm just making it worse, aren't I?"

Tears threatened, but she refused to let them fall. "It wouldn't be the same. That other ring... It was part of the Cinderella Ball, part of how we met." She gave a forlorn shrug. "I don't think I can explain."

Jake shut his eyes. She didn't have to explain. He understood better than she knew. She was hurting and there wasn't a damned thing he could do about it. She wouldn't agree to a replacement and he didn't have a hope in hell of recovering the original.

He thought about it all through that long afternoon as he worked outside with his ranch hands, setting a grueling work schedule for himself in the vain hope of easing his guilt. Toward the end of the day, a possible solution occurred to him, one he filed away for future consideration.

"Ready to call it a day?" Dusty finally asked, "or haven't you punished yourself enough?"

Jake lifted an eyebrow in question. "The men complaining?"

"Not yet. But that's not why I'm asking." Dusty stared pointedly toward the north. "Any man who doesn't keep one eye on the weather is just askin' for trouble."

Jake followed the direction of his foreman's gaze, then stowed his tools and went in search of Wynne. He found her in the library. "Come with me. I have something to show you," he said.

She looked up from her book. "What is it?"

"Ever seen a blue norther?" he asked, tugging her from the chair.

She laughed. "I don't even know what it is."

"It's a weather front. A rather impressive weather front."

He walked out onto the front porch with her and pointed north. "That's a blue norther."

A broad bank of steel-blue clouds chewed at the horizon. Even as she watched the ominous ridge consumed still more of the crystalline sky, roiling toward them like some airborne blight.

She shivered. "Is it serious?"

"Can be if you're not paying attention. Northers come in fast and hit hard. One minute it'll be seventy, the next near freezing. Top that with a nasty wind and chilly rain and—"

"And I better have the boys pull out some warm clothing."

"Good idea." He snagged the collar of her shirt and tugged her closer, his golden eyes glittering with wicked intent. "I think this calls for another fire, don't you? That way you won't need to bother with warm clothes. Hell, you won't need to bother with any clothes at all."

She gave him an innocent look. "How in the world will I keep warm?"

"I'll think of something," he replied, grinning. "After dinner, how about we get the boys settled for the night, open up a bottle of wine and celebrate the coming of an early winter?"

She slid her arms around his waist, settling into the cradle of his hips. "What sort of celebration did you have in mind?"

"We can try one of those pagan rituals. You know, the ones where the participants are all buck-naked and chase each other around in circles. You can play the woodland nymph and I'll be the wicked satyr."

She moistened her lips. "I thought that was a springtime ritual."

"Okay." His mouth nuzzled the side of her neck. "We'll also pretend it's March."

Her eyes drifted closed and a helpless moan slipped from her throat. "Call the boys and I'll get dinner started."

He pushed her collar to one side, baring a creamy shoulder. "I thought they were in the house with you." She stiffened beneath his hands and he pulled back. "They're not?"

She shook her head, apprehension reflected in her eyes. "They said—they said they were going to help you."

"When?" He shot the word at her.

"Hours ago," she whispered. "Right after Mrs. Marsh—"

He swore. Pushing past her, he charged into the house, taking the steps to the boys' bedroom two at a time.

Even before he found the note, he knew they'd run. Dresser drawers hung open, clothes formed a telltale trail from closet to bed. And most telling of all, the picture of their parents was missing from the nightstand.

Wynne entered the room behind him. He watched as she crossed to Buster's pillow and picked up the note. She read silently, covering her mouth with a trembling hand. Then she turned and walked into his arms.

"We'll find them," he tried to reassure. She felt so cold, as though all the zest and life had been frozen into an impenetrable ball of ice. Briskly he ran his hands up and down her arms. "I'll organize the men. They can't have gotten far."

"You said those fronts move in fast. How long do we have?"

"A couple hours," he lied without hesitation.

They wasted thirty minutes searching the house and outbuildings. It didn't surprise anyone that the boys were nowhere to be found. Jake pulled Dusty to one side, speaking fast, his face set in grim lines. "Have the men mount up and fan out," he said, glancing at the sky. "That front's moving in faster than I'd anticipated. We don't have much time."

"Why don't I drive over to Lost Trail and see if they're holed up there?" Dusty offered.

"Good idea."

"Jake—"

"I know. I'll take care of it." Without another word, he turned and headed for the house. He'd delayed long enough. Now he had to act. For the first time in his life, he was going to ask for assistance. He only prayed the people of Chesterfield would be willing to give it. Snatching up the phone, he punched in a number.

"Belle Blue here. What can I do you for?"

"It's Jake Hondo." He took a deep breath and said, "Belle, I need help."

Dead silence met his request. "You want help?" she repeated. "You, Jake?"

He gritted his teeth. "Yeah, me."

If she found his request amusing, she hid it well. "Sure thing. What's the problem?"

"It's the boys. They've run off."

"Oh, my heavens," she said with a gasp. "Jake, there's a norther movin' in."

"I know that!" He closed his eyes, struggling just this once to keep his temper in check. "Will you round up a search party for me? We need to find those boys. Fast."

"Consider it done. And Jake?" She spoke with more warmth than he'd ever heard before. "Don't you and your missus worry none. We'll track 'em down."

"Thanks," he whispered and cradled the receiver. He didn't doubt for a minute the boys would be found. The question was . . . Would it be in time?

CHAPTER TEN

EVENING HAD SET IN when the door to the kitchen opened. Wynne watched anxiously as Jake stepped across the threshold and tossed aside his rain-soaked Stetson. He shook his head in answer to her silent query.

She turned away, fighting for control. "What are we going to do, Jake?"

"What else can we do?" Exhaustion filled his voice. "We keep looking."

Her hands balled in frustration. "It doesn't make sense that they haven't shown up. The boys may be foolhardy, but they're not stupid. They wouldn't stay out in this weather. What about Lost Trail? Perhaps they—"

"Dusty searched it earlier."

"It's a long walk." Desperation tainted her words. "Maybe they weren't there, yet. Or maybe they hid from him."

"Okay," he said evenly. "I'll go check the house again."

She turned around, setting her chin at a defiant angle. "I'm going with you."

To her surprise, he didn't argue. Perhaps he knew how desperately she needed to act, to do more than wait, worry and brew coffee for the search party. "Get coats," he instructed. "And some blankets. If we find them, they're going to be half-frozen."

Jake's broken hand prevented him from driving a stick shift, so Wynne slid behind the steering wheel of the truck. Not wasting any time, she started the engine, ground into first gear and spun out of the driveway.

Fifteen minutes later she pulled into the dirt road leading to Lost Trail. Jake leaned forward, peering through the windshield.

"Aw, hell! Floor it, Wynne. I see a light."

She stomped on the accelerator, shooting off the end of the driveway and bouncing heedlessly across the lawn. Skidding to a halt outside the mudroom door, she leapt from the truck and raced into the house. The sight that greeted her almost brought her to her knees. A fitful fire crackled in the grate of the wood-burning stove, throwing off a miserly warmth. The boys sat huddled on the kitchen floor in front of it.

They weren't moving.

"Buster? Chick?" she called, approaching with leaden feet, afraid of what she'd find. They shifted in response to the sound of her voice and she sent up a silent prayer of relief—until they turned around. She gasped in horror at their pale, blue-tinged complexions.

"Hi, Aunt Wynne," Buster murmured in an exhausted little voice. "Boy, are we glad to see you."

She fell on them, hugging them close. "Me, too," she answered, her voice breaking despite her best efforts. They were cold. So very cold.

"We tried to call, but the phone didn't work."

Jake came in then, dropping blankets and coats at their feet and Chick held up his arms. "Uncle Dad," he whispered, croaking out the first words he'd spoken aloud in a long, long time. "I knew you would gets me."

It was too much to bear. In the darkest moments of despair, a miracle was born. Wynne bowed her head and burst into tears.

Jake scooped up Chick, his hands trembling uncontrollably, and buried his face in the boy's silky hair. "Go start the truck and turn the heater on high while I wrap them up," he ordered tersely. "We need to get them to the hospital as soon as possible."

"Are they going to be all right?" she questioned anxiously.

"I hope so." Moving with swift efficiency, he carried Chick from the house. Then he returned for Buster, situating the boys so they were close to the heating vents of the truck. "Let's go."

She tried to force the clutch into gear, but stalled the engine. For the first time ever, Jake heard her swear. He caught her hand as she reached for the ignition, his steady, golden gaze holding hers. "Take it easy, honey. I know you're frightened. But it'll work out. I promise."

"I can't. I can't do it," she cried. "He's finally talking and I can't hold it together long enough—"

"They're safe," Jake said calmly. "We just have to get them to a doctor to make sure they aren't suffering from exposure."

"We're safe now, Aunt Wynne," Buster repeated sleepily. "You don't have to be scared no more."

"No more," Chick confirmed.

"Now slow and easy, just like I taught you," Jake said. "Remember? First gear is a kiss."

She nodded, fighting off tears. Taking a deep breath, she turned the key and restarted the truck. This time, she slid smoothly into first.

"Thatta girl. Now a gentle touch."

Pushing in the clutch, she shifted into second. "How far to the hospital?"

"The closest one is in Two Forks."

"Jake—"

"Don't panic. You can do it. Shift into third."

"A bolder touch," she recited in a shaky voice.

"That's right. You're doing fine. Now drop down to a gentle touch as we take this curve. Well done."

He continued to talk the entire way. First helping her through the gears, then encouraging the boys. His voice was all that saved her from insanity. Pulling up to the emergency doors, it took three tries to peel her white-knuckled hands off the steering wheel. By the time she climbed from the truck, the boys had been taken inside.

"The doctors are looking at your sons now, Mrs. Hondo," a nurse advised. "In the meantime, I have some forms for you to fill out." While Wynne wrote and worried and waited for word on the boys' condition, Jake went to the pay phones to call off the search party.

"They were all out there looking," he said when he rejoined her. "Every last man. Even Randolph."

"They're not bad people," she replied. "You just need to give them half a chance."

"You think they'd let me?"

A smile slid across her mouth. "Yes. I think they would."

Thirty minutes later, the doctor entered the waiting room. "Good news, folks. Your boys check out fine. It might have been a different story, if the oldest hadn't been smart enough to build a fire. They got lucky."

"May we see them?" Wynne requested.

"Of course. We're going to keep them overnight just for observation. But you can visit for a while, if you'd like."

The boys had been put in the pediatric ward, their beds side by side. Wynne climbed in with Chick, holding him so tightly he squirmed in protest. Jake sat with Buster.

"You mad?" the boy questioned nervously.

Jake didn't bother to pull his punches. "Sure am. Care to explain why you took off like that?"

"We heard Aunt Marsh say she was going to take us away. So I thought we oughta hide till she went home."

"I guess that means you don't trust your Uncle Jake," Wynne spoke up.

Buster stared at her in confusion. "What?"

She returned his look, her gaze cool and serious. "You should have trusted him to keep his promise. He said he'd protect us from Aunt Marsh and he will."

"Wynne," Jake began. "I don't think—"

"It's important that they know." She cut him off. "When you say you're going to do something, they need to trust you." She scrutinized first one boy, then the other. "Understood?"

Chick snuggled deeper into her arms. "Okay," he answered without hesitation.

"I'm sorry I didn't believe you, Uncle Jake," Buster said contritely. "It won't never happen again."

His hands firmly tied, Jake leaned against the headboard and closed his eyes. Now what the hell did he do?

Mrs. Marsh appeared on their doorstep first thing the next morning.

She breezed into the house as though she owned it, commanding immediate attention. "I heard what happened to my nephews," she began without preamble.

"And ran right over to see how they were," Jake finished for her.

Her mouth twisted. "Cute, but wrong. I'm here to issue an ultimatum."

"Another one?" Wynne couldn't help asking.

"A final one. You see, thanks to this latest episode, there's no question that I'll win custody of the boys. You've put the children at risk too many times. So I'm giving you one more—"

"Get to the point." Jake cut her off.

Her gaze grew stony with dislike. "Very well. You had a quickie Nevada marriage, now I want you to get a quickie Mexican divorce. You do that, and not only will I grant Wynne generous visitation rights, I'll put it in writing. Fight me for so much as another day and she'll never see them again." She paused, flashing sharklike teeth. "You'll understand if I require an immediate answer."

He knew what he'd like to tell her. But one glance at Wynne, one glimpse of the fear and panic she fought so hard to hide, put paid to that idea. Besides, he didn't want open warfare with the Marsh woman. Not yet. Not when another option was available—a choice that had to be one of the toughest he'd ever faced.

"Well?" she prompted impatiently.

His hands clenched. "My marriage in exchange for the kids, is that how it works?"

"That's it."

"I'll agree—on one condition."

"*Jake, no!*" Tears sprang to Wynne's eyes, tears she brushed aside with an impatient hand. "Don't do it."

"Name your condition," Mrs. Marsh said quickly. It was obvious she sensed an easy victory.

"I need time."

She inclined her head. "Very well. I'll give you three days."

"It might take longer."

"Don't let it," she retorted with curt finality. "You have money. Use it. These matters can be taken care of easily enough ... for the right price."

"Trust you to know that," he muttered. "Oh, and there's one other condition. I'll fly out today, but I need your promise that you won't act until my return."

"I'll hold off for three days and not a second longer. Do we have a deal?"

"I guess you could call it that."

She heaved an exaggerated sigh of relief. "Well! That wasn't so difficult. It certainly has been a pleasure doing business with you, Mr. Hondo."

"Not from where I'm standin'."

She flashed her dimples. "Next time we meet I expect it to be with divorce papers in hand. Don't disappoint

me, now. You wouldn't want to make me angry."
Throwing Wynne a look of triumph, she sailed from the
room.

Silence reigned for a full minute. Jake stared at the
floor, steeling himself to deal with the tears, the disillusionment, the pleas.

"Jake—"

He stopped her with a single look. "We don't have
any choice, you realize that, don't you? We have to settle
the issue of our marriage once and for all."

"But—"

He shook his head. "I don't want to hear it. Those
boys have to come first. Do you want to lose them completely? Your dragon-lady isn't fooling around. She's
desperate, and as much as I'd like to deny it, she has a
case."

"You promised," she whispered. "We had an
agreement."

"I promised to take care of your dragon and that's
what I'll do. But it has to be my way."

She started to speak, then hesitated. Instead she took
a step closer, then another and another until she stopped
right in front of him. And all the while she stared as
though she could see straight through to his soul. Questions danced within her unflinching gaze, trembled on
her lips. But she didn't speak them. Even as he watched
a quiet conviction slipped across her face, absolute trust
a flame in the verdant green of her eyes.

Finally she nodded. "I'll let you take care of it," was
all she said.

"That's it?" he demanded. "No questions? No
complaints?"

She managed a shaky smile. "Would it do any good?"

"No."

She clasped her hands together, her fingers uncon-
sciously searching for a wedding band that was forever

lost. The minute awareness struck, she dropped her arms to her sides. "If you're going to be gone for three days, you'll need some clothes. Why don't I help you pack?"

"Thanks," he said gruffly. "I'd appreciate that. I'd like to speak to the boys first, though."

It didn't take long. After explaining to Buster and Chick that he was leaving on a business trip, Jake crossed to the bedroom he shared with his wife and pulled an overnight bag from the closet. Pawing through his dresser, he threw the bare essentials into the case. Wynne went right behind him, removing and folding each item before repacking it.

Finished, he turned and glanced at her. "It's time."

Her chin wobbled ever so slightly. "Have a safe trip. I'll see you in a few days." She flashed him an anxious look. "Right?"

"Yeah, you'll see me again." He picked up his suitcase and took a step toward the door, but found he couldn't leave her, not like this. His case hit the ground. "Come here."

She ran into his arms, almost knocking him over. She was steel cloaked in velvet, a delicate beauty built over indomitable strength. The breath shuddered though her as she gathered that strength, slipping her hands across the tense muscles of his chest. Her lips skimmed his cheek like a butterfly, then honed in on his mouth. With a dark groan, he kissed her, pillaging the generous warmth with a desperation she couldn't mistake. Finally he set her from him.

"I have to go."

She didn't speak, simply nodded.

He picked up his bag and this time, made it to the door. At the threshold, he hesitated, his back to her. "Do you trust me, elf?"

"I always have," came her choked response. "And I always will."

His voice dropped, sounding raspy and strained. "I've never had anyone trust me before."

He barely caught her answer. "That's because you've never been married to me before."

His shoulders sagged beneath the burden of her words. "You have no idea the risk you're taking," he informed her harshly.

And then he was gone.

Judge Graydon pounded his gavel, bringing the court to order. A silence settled over the packed room as everyone eagerly waited for the proceedings to begin.

"I'm afraid we've delayed long enough," the judge said, looking at Wynne. "Have you heard from Jake, yet?"

Reluctantly she shook her head. "I'm afraid not."

There hadn't been a word from him, not in all of the five impossibly long days that had passed since he'd left. During that time, she'd build a protective wall around her emotions, allowing nothing to intrude—except for her nephews. And all the while she'd clung to her hope and her faith, discovering in the deepest hours of the night that faith and hope made for very cold bedfellows.

The judge sighed. "Then we'll have to begin without him. But I want it clearly understood that this is not a legal proceeding." He glared first at Peter, who sat next to her, then at the dapper lawyer who'd escorted Mrs. Marsh into the courtroom. "We're just having a nice, friendlylike discussion in order see if there's room for a compromise."

The dapper lawyer popped to his feet. "Larry Livingston, Jr., Your Honor. And I can assure you there isn't any room at all."

Graydon pointed his gavel at the man. "Sit down and stay put. I'll let you know if I'm interested in your opinion. Understood?"

Deflated, the lawyer did as he was told. "Understood, Your Honor."

"Good. Now I've reviewed Mrs. Marsh's complaints." The judge's brows pulled together. "And I don't think anyone can deny that these incidents she's detailed actually happened. Heck-fire, Jake himself told me about the run-in the boys had with Mad Dog and that rattler."

Livingston springboarded to his feet again. "Your Honor, I object. Your relationship with the defendant is a clear-cut conflict of interest. I request—"

"Sit down!" Judge Graydon thundered. "I've already told you this is just a friendly little discussion, not a legal proceeding."

"But, Your Honor—"

Graydon leaned across the bench. "Let me offer you a piece of advice, Mr. Livingston. Since I'm the only judge in town, I suggest you do your level best *not* to tick me off. It won't help your client any. Got it?"

Livingston gulped, subsiding into his chair once more. "Got it, Your Honor."

Peter cleared his throat. "If I may?"

"If you must. Keep it brief, Bryant."

"Yes, Your Honor. I'd just like to say that . . . boys will be boys."

Graydon snorted. "Quite insightful of you, Petey. Only these incidents are a little more serious than that."

"It isn't just the danger." Mrs. Marsh spoke up, managing to sound genuinely concerned. "Although, as you say, that's serious enough. But when you combine it with the problems surrounding Wynne's marriage, I just don't see how anyone can believe my nephews would be better off with her."

The judge lifted an eyebrow. "And what problems would those be?" he asked.

Impossibly long lashes swept downward to conceal the expression in her eyes. "Everyone knows their relationship is a sham. He only married her to get his hands on Chesterfield Ranch.'' She glanced around as though for support. "Surely it's no secret. Just as it's no secret that he's going to divorce her.'' Her tone sharpened. "And once he does, she'll have no husband, no home and no viable means of support.''

Graydon frowned. "I've never put much credence in gossip, Mrs. Marsh. Nor should you. As far as I know, there's been no talk of a divorce.''

She smiled smugly. "Yes, there has. In fact, that's why he isn't here. He's getting a divorce even as we speak.''

The courtroom erupted.

"Wait a minute!'' the judge shouted. "Quiet!'' He banged his gavel until the ruckus had died down. Then he fixed a stern gaze on Mrs. Marsh. "Are you telling this court you know where Jake is?''

"I suggest you try Mexico,'' she replied, studying her perfectly manicured nails. "Or possibly Haiti. Wherever he can get a quick divorce. Though considering how long he's been gone, I'd hardly call it quick.''

Judge Graydon switched his attention to Wynne. "Did you know Jake was off getting a divorce?''

"No,'' she answered politely. "Because he's not.''

"Well, now I'm confused. One says he is and the other says he isn't.'' He released a gusty sigh. "Let's get this sorted out.''

Toward the back of the room, Randolph stood. "Excuse me, Your Honor. May I say something?''

"I don't believe we need your brand of help, Chesterfield,'' the judge retorted.

"I actually planned to speak on Jake's behalf.'' He held up his hands at the hoots of disbelief from the people seated around him. "I know, I know. That's a first for me. But I recently discovered that I've been wrong about him, that I've accused him of things he

never did." He took a deep breath. "My...my cousin
never laid a finger on Evie, despite what I may have told
folks in the past. It was just a big misunderstanding. I
saw him drop her off one night, heard her crying and
naturally assumed... Well, the bottom line is, I was
wrong. Evie tried to explain at the time, but I didn't
believe her. I guess I wanted to think the worst of Jake.
Y'all can probably figure out why."

"What changed your mind?" Wynne asked.

"You did," he confessed. "And Evie. The way you
both defended him. After dinner last week my wife got
rather...vocal on the subject. It was enough to make
me stop and listen." He folded his arms across his chest,
reminding her vividly of Jake. "I guess what I'm sayin'
is... I'm not willing to jump to any more conclusions
about the man. If Wynne says he's not divorcing her,
Jake will have to say different before I'll believe it." And
with that, he sat down.

"Nice speech," Judge Graydon approved. "But that
doesn't change the fact that Jake isn't here and we have
conflicting reports regarding his intentions. Wynne, I
hate to ask this, but... What exactly did he say to you
before he left?"

"Do I have to answer that?" she whispered.

"I'm afraid so, my dear."

"He said..." She clasped her hands together, searching
again for a ring that wasn't there. Taking a deep breath,
she confessed, "He said that he didn't have any choice.
He was going to settle the issue of our marriage once
and for all."

A shocked murmur rippled through the room.

"And that didn't suggest to you that Jake is planning
a divorce?" Judge Graydon questioned gently.

She shook her head, a stubborn light leaping to her
eyes. "I trust Jake. He wouldn't do that to me. He knows
I need a husband if I'm to keep the children."

A man in the back of the courtroom stood, twisting his Stetson between his hands. "Excuse me, Judge. But if all she needs is a husband, I'll volunteer. And I wouldn't marry her and then change my mind after the fact, neither."

"Kind of you to offer, Wendall," Graydon began. "But—"

Another man stood. "I wouldn't object to having a wife like Miz Hondo. If Jake don't come through, I'm willing to offer for her."

Three more men stood. The judge ran a hand across his face. "Let me guess. You, too?" he asked. They all nodded. "It would seem you have no shortage of husbands to choose from, Mrs. Hondo."

"Just not the one I want," she replied, her voice catching.

Asa Blue rose to his feet. "Jake's divorcing Wynne and that's a fact. We all know the man. We all know why he married. And we all know he intended to divorce his missus once he was legally wedded, bedded and court-approved."

No one argued with his assessment of the situation.

"So, let's get to the crux of the matter," he continued. "Wynne says the children were left to her in her sister's will. The Marsh lady says that without a husband, a home or a job, the children would be better off with her. Makes sense to me that if we get Wynne what she needs, then there won't be any more problems."

Murmurs of agreement echoed around the courtroom.

"Now, here's what I propose." Asa ticked off on his fingers. "Belle and I will make sure she has a job. As far as a home is concerned . . . Either she can live with her new husband or we'll rent her a place in town. That just leaves gettin' her a man." He planted his hands on his hips and scanned the room. "All you who are interested in applying for the position of her husband, stand up so she can pick out the one she likes best.''

''Wait just a damned minute,'' Mrs. Marsh snapped, leaping to her feet. ''This is insane.''

Judge Graydon cocked an eyebrow. ''How so? You've listed your complaints and we're taking care of them for you.''

''There's one small problem,'' Wynne interrupted. ''*I* haven't agreed.''

''But, honey,'' Belle called out. ''What Asa's suggesting is the perfect solution.''

Wynne turned to face her. ''Except . . . Jake and I are still married.''

''For your sake, I'd like to believe that's true,'' Belle replied compassionately. ''But you have to be realistic. You know what sort of man Jake is. And you know he only wanted a temporary marriage. Heck, his own words condemn him. As tough as it is, there comes a time when you have to face facts.''

Wynne looked around. Except for Randolph, they all returned her gaze with pitying looks. She bowed her head. ''You're right,'' she said softly. ''When you weigh all the evidence, I have to admit, there isn't much room for doubt. Chances are, Jake's going to divorce me.''

In the back of the courtroom, shadowed in the doorway, stood Jake. He caught the arm of the woman next to him before she could reveal their presence. ''Quiet,'' he murmured. ''Let her finish.''

''But—''

His eyes flashed an unmistakable warning. ''For once in your life, shut the hell up.''

He returned his attention to the scene being played out before him and folded his arms across his chest. His wife sat near the front of the silent courtroom, her head still bowed. Wisps of white-blond hair clung to her nape and more than anything he wanted to go to her, slide his hands into those silky curls and kiss her senseless. But he didn't move. He simply stood and waited, steadfast in his conviction.

After a full minute, Wynne lifted her chin. "It's obvious to everyone here he's going to divorce me," she reiterated, then stated in a firm, carrying voice, "But I still don't believe it. I think you're all wrong. I think he loves me. And I know I love him. So until he walks in here and hands me the actual divorce papers, I'll have to decline your generous offers. But I appreciate your support."

It was all he needed to hear. Dragging his companion along with him, he strode into the courtroom, never once looking right or left. The entire time he kept his gaze trained on the only person in the world who mattered to him. He stopped in front of her and without a word yanked her from the chair and into his arms. And then he kissed her. He kissed her as if there was no yesterday and no tomorrow, kissed her with all the pent-up passion of a man who'd lived a life of emptiness and despair, kissed her until the darkness of the past few days had been vanquished from her soul.

He felt her hot tears on his cheeks, tasted the sweetness of her love, heard the glorious sound of his name tumbling over and over from her lips to his. "I love you," he whispered for her ears alone. "And I swear, I'll never give you cause to doubt me again."

"Excuse me!" Mrs. Marsh's jarring voice cut like a knife. "Perhaps we can get back to business?"

Jake turned, planting himself between Wynne and her dragon. "Sure thing. Mind telling me what the hell is going on here?"

"We're picking out a husband for your wife," a voice called from the far side of the courtroom.

Jake's eyes flashed dangerously. "My wife already has a husband, she doesn't need another."

"*What*?" Bright patches of red stained Kitty Marsh's cheeks. "You said you were getting a divorce! We had an agreement."

"What agreement is this?" Judge Graydon interrupted.

She blanched, as though aware she'd said far too much. "I...I don't think that's relevant," she stammered.

The judge's eyes narrowed. "I suspect it's very relevant. But we'll get back to that later." He switched his attention to Jake. "Mind answering a question or two, Hondo?"

Jake lounged against the defendant's table, his arms folded across his chest. "Ask away," he said with a shrug.

"We seem to have rumors of a divorce floating around here. I don't suppose you'd care to give us the straight poop."

Jake managed to look suitably shocked. "A divorce? You mean, me?" He fixed the Marsh woman with a cold, feral gaze. "Who the hell said I was getting a divorce?"

The judge glanced at Mrs. Marsh, as well, his expression souring. "Rumor had it you were off to Mexico."

"Actually, it was Nevada."

"Well, I know for a fact you can't get a divorce in Nevada, not in just five days. What were you doing there? If you don't mind my asking, that is."

"I don't mind." He tugged two small, wrapped packages from his pocket. "I was buying my wife a couple of presents."

Judge Graydon leaned across the bench. "You spent the last five days in Nevada buying your wife a gift?"

Jake shrugged. "Couldn't get them anywhere else. And they were important gifts."

Wynne peeked eagerly around his shoulder. "May I open them? Now?"

He smiled indulgently. "Yeah, elf. Go ahead." He handed her the first—a small, square jeweler's box.

She ripped off the ribbon and paper and slowly flipped up the red velvet lid. Inside were a pair of wedding bands. Very unique, strangely etched wedding bands. "Oh, Jake," she whispered.

"Know what they're made from?"

She nodded, struggling to talk through her tears. "From the tickets to the Cinderella Ball."

He cupped her cheek, lifting her chin so he could see the expression in her eyes as he said, "You told me your ring couldn't be replaced because it was part of the ball, part of how we met."

Understanding dawned. "And so is this." She touched the larger band, moistening her lips. "There's two of them."

"About time I wore one, don't you think?" He removed the rings and slid the smaller onto her finger. "Don't go losing it. I had a hell of a time convincing the Montagues to part with even one of their precious tickets."

Then it was her turn. She took his hand in hers and gently, firmly slid the band onto his finger. "You're not a temporary husband anymore, are you?"

He shook his head. "I don't think I ever was. But just in case there are any lingering doubts." He handed her the second present, a small, flat package.

She opened it, gasping when she saw a familiar, white velvet pouch. Inside were two tickets, the words *Anniversary Ball* etched in elegant scrollwork on the golden metallic wafers. Tears fell, thick and furious.

Jake straightened and faced the rest of the courtroom, his face settling into savage, uncompromising lines. "Anybody have more questions about the validity of my marriage? If so, they can come up here and discuss them with me close and personal.''

"This doesn't change anything," Mrs. Marsh insisted shrilly. "There's still the question of my nephews' safety. He's a dangerous man. Just look at his hand. I don't even want to think about how he broke it. Probably in a fistfight or something."

The judge grinned. "How did you break it, Jake?"

"Fishing for Wynne's wedding ring," he admitted reluctantly.

"Come again?"

"She'd dropped her ring down the drain and I couldn't get the pipe off, so..." He shrugged.

"You lost your temper and tried to force the issue."

"Something like that." He ran a hand through his hair. "She was crying. I—I couldn't just stand there and do nothing."

"Faced with that choice, I suppose a busted hand is understandable. So is a five-day trip to Nevada." Graydon shook his head. "The things we men do to make our wives happy."

There were a few sympathetic chuckles from the audience.

"I guess that leaves one final issue," the judge said, turning a stern eye on Mrs. Marsh.

"Your Honor—" she began.

"My turn." Judge Graydon cut her off. "Madam, I'd like to offer a few words of advice. You are, of course, welcome to pursue legal action against these people. But I strongly suggest you reconsider. Because I promise, should you take this any further I will make it my personal business to find out about this mysterious agreement Jake referred to. And when I do, I'll be sure to forward that information to the appropriate parties." He let that sink in before adding, "Enjoy the rest of your visit to Texas. I trust it will be a brief one."

The courtroom exploded with applause.

Wynne stared up at her husband, her heart in her eyes. "I love you," she said. "Thank you."

"And I must love you something fierce," he admitted wryly. "Otherwise I wouldn't have brought *her* with me." He jerked his head toward someone standing out of sight.

Wynne turned. "Laura!" she cried, throwing her arms around her best friend. "What are you doing here?"

"Your husband can be very persuasive when he sets his mind to it. And he persuaded me I should give Texas another try."

People began to drift over to them, offering their congratulations and saying a few kind words in the hope of making amends. But it was to only one man that Jake offered his hand. "Thanks for what you said, cousin. I appreciate it."

Randolph shrugged awkwardly. "Family should stick together."

Jake wrapped his arm around his wife and grinned, the last of his demons finally conquered. "I couldn't agree more. How about you and Evie joining us for Thanksgiving dinner? We have a lot to celebrate."

EPILOGUE

WYNNE GLANCED at the people gathered for Thanksgiving dinner and smiled mistily. She'd never thought she'd be so fortunate, or have so much to be thankful for. Jake met her gaze across the long expanse of the table and winked. Then, breaking off his conversation with Randolph, he lifted his glass.

"I'd like to propose a toast," he said. He looked at Wynne, his eyes gleaming like polished gold in the candlelight. "To you, elf. I've never been more grateful for anything in my life."

There was a momentary silence and then Randolph lifted his glass. "And to Jake. I'm thankful for having the opportunity to finally straighten out our differences. I'm especially thankful he sold some of his land to me. And though I wouldn't have minded getting my hands on Chesterfield Ranch..." He grinned to let everyone know he was just kidding.

"He's happy to settle for a parcel of fine riverfront acreage instead," Evie finished for him. "And so am I."

Laura lifted her glass next, sending Peter a blatantly besotted look. "Well, I can't tell you how thankful I am to discover that Texas men aren't nearly as bad as I remember."

"Here, here," Peter said, shooting her an equally besotted look. "And I can't tell you how grateful I am to hear her say that."

Buster grabbed his glass of milk and hefted it with two hands. "I'm thankful, too, 'cause Jake slewed our dragon."

All eyes turned to Chick, and Wynne sent up a silent prayer. Slowly he popped his thumb from his mouth. "I's thankful I can talk," he announced in a clear, piping voice.

After the laughter had died, Jake glanced at Wynne. "And what about you? What are you thankful for?"

A slow, radiant smile crept across her mouth. "I'm thankful that this house has a nursery."

Seven sets of eyes pivoted in her direction, reflecting various degrees of shock.

Then Jake said, "You mean—"

* * * * *

*Look out next month for ACCIDENTAL WIFE,
the second book in Day Leclaire's
wonderful trilogy.*

Free Gift Offer

With a Free Gift proof-of-purchase
from any Harlequin® book, you can receive
a beautiful cubic zirconia pendant.

This stunning marquise-shaped stone is a genuine cubic
zirconia—accented by an 18" gold tone necklace.
(Approximate retail value $19.95)

Send for yours today...

compliments of ◈HARLEQUIN®

To receive your free gift, a cubic zirconia pendant, send us one original proof-of-purchase, photocopies not accepted, from the back of any Harlequin Romance®, Harlequin Presents®, Harlequin Temptation®, Harlequin Superromance®, Harlequin Intrigue®, Harlequin American Romance®, or Harlequin Historicals® title available in August, September or October at your favorite retail outlet, together with the Free Gift Certificate, plus a check or money order for $1.65 U.S./$2.15 CAN. (do not send cash) to cover postage and handling, payable to Harlequin Free Gift Offer. We will send you the specified gift. Allow 6 to 8 weeks for delivery. Offer good until December 31, 1996, or while quantities last. Offer valid in the U.S. and Canada only.

Free Gift Certificate

Name: _____

Address: _____

City: _____ State/Province: _____ Zip/Postal Code: _____

Mail this certificate, one proof-of-purchase and a check or money order for postage and handling to: HARLEQUIN FREE GIFT OFFER 1996. In the U.S.: 3010 Walden Avenue, P.O. Box 9071, Buffalo NY 14269-9057. In Canada: P.O. Box 604, Fort Erie, Ontario L2Z 5X3.

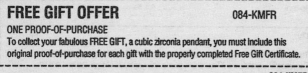

FREE GIFT OFFER

084-KMFR

ONE PROOF-OF-PURCHASE
To collect your fabulous FREE GIFT, a cubic zirconia pendant, you must include this
original proof-of-purchase for each gift with the properly completed Free Gift Certificate.

084-KMFR

Take 4 bestselling love stories FREE

Plus get a FREE surprise gift!

Special Limited-time Offer

Mail to Harlequin Reader Service®

3010 Walden Avenue
P.O. Box 1867
Buffalo, N.Y. 14240-1867

YES! Please send me 4 free Harlequin Romance® novels and my free surprise gift. Then send me 6 brand-new novels every month, which I will receive months before they appear in bookstores. Bill me at the low price of $2.67 each plus 25¢ delivery and applicable sales tax if any*. That's the complete price and a savings of over 10% off the cover prices—quite a bargain! I understand that accepting the books and gift places me under no obligation ever to buy any books. I can always return a shipment and cancel at any time. Even if I never buy another book from Harlequin, the 4 free books and the surprise gift are mine to keep forever.

116 BPA A3UK

Name	(PLEASE PRINT)	
Address	Apt. No.	
City	State	Zip

This offer is limited to one order per household and not valid to present Harlequin Romance® subscribers. *Terms and prices are subject to change without notice. Sales tax applicable in N.Y.

UROM-696   ©1990 Harlequin Enterprises Limited

You're About to Become a

 *Privileged Woman*

Reap the rewards of fabulous free gifts and benefits with proofs-of-purchase from Harlequin and Silhouette books

Pages & Privileges™

It's our way of thanking you for buying our books at your favorite retail stores.

PROOF OF PURCHASE

HR-PP19

Offer expires March 31, 1997

Harlequin and Silhouette—
the most privileged readers in the world!

For more information about Harlequin and Silhouette's PAGES & PRIVILEGES program call the Pages & Privileges Benefits Desk: 1-503-794-2499

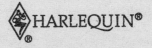 HARLEQUIN®

HR-PP19